The Janeite's Dream Book of Trivia:
750 Questions about Jane Austen's works, life, and influence

Tiffany Bascom & Trudy Wallis

ISBN: 978-0-9969478-7-9

Jane Austen is our heroine! We just can't get enough of her wit and genius. She teaches us to laugh at ourselves. We grow along with her characters. We fall in love again and again. Nothing can compare to the way Austen's stories spark our sensibilities and keep us wishing for more. As we find ourselves desperate to revive Jane so that she can finish all of her novels and write several more, we are left grasping for new ways to enjoy her works. Whatever we want to call ourselves—Janeites, Austenites, Austenphiles, Jane Austen Lovers—the description is apt. We love Jane Austen!

This collection of 750 trivia questions aims to be COMPREHENSIVE. We researched her works, her life, and the influence she has had over other authors and media. The questions are for self-testing and study, as well as group discussion and challenges. Do you know where James Morland proposed to Isabella Thorpe? Do you know which character is obsessed with looking glasses? Do you know the name of Jane Austen's cottage? It's time to see how much of a Janeite you are!

We researched and mixed the questions well to touch on all areas of the Jane Austen world. We "shuffled" five different types of questions so they could be used in playing trivia games (more on that later). They range in difficulty from "no sweat" to "Huh?" This is a great time to fill in the gaps if you haven't studied Jane Austen as well as you'd like.

Here are the five question types:

	Book Question: tests you on plot points and details
	Character Quip: tests your knowledge of quotes *by* or *about* a character

	Jane's Life and Times: tests you on Jane's life and the world she lived in
	Jane in Other Media: tests your knowledge of movies, books, plays, music, etc. that she influenced
	Regarding Jane: tests what you know of other writers' opinions of Jane

We have divided the questions into 30 sections of 25 questions each. We did this so you can test yourself on one section at a time. How many you get right depends on how much of a Janeite you are.

21-25 questions correct: true Janeite!

16-20: a Janeite in your heart, but not a true proficient

11-15: a Janeite about to bloom

6-10: you've only watched the movies, haven't you?

1-5: start reading *now*

GAMES

There are many ways to use these trivia questions to play games. Here are a couple ideas.

Trivial Pursuit

Simply toss out the usual trivia question box and use the questions in this collection. Don't worry about which category you land on. You get a "pie piece" when you answer the next question correctly on the "pie piece" square. Once you've filled up your pie with each color, you win.

Trivia (Party Game)

This is fun for book clubs or other Jane-related gatherings. Get some small whiteboards, one per person or team. Ask a question of the whole group. (You may want to eliminate the answer options if the question would be too easy for that group of players.) Players cannot shout out answers, just write them down on the whiteboards before 30 seconds have elapsed. Whichever person/team has the correct answer on their board receives a point. When you've reached the end of a set number of questions, reward the winner(s). Alternatively, you may give points to the person/team that answers the question correctly in the least amount of time.

Enjoy your journey!

Sincerely,

The Writers

1. Which city, known for its healing mineral waters, is featured in two of Jane Austen's novels?

Set 1

Answers on pg. 159

2. Whom does this describe?
"She had two daughters, both of whom she had lived to see respectably married, and she now therefore had nothing to do but marry the rest of the world."

A) Mrs. Jennings (*Sense and Sensibility*)
B) Mrs. Allen (*Northanger Abbey*)
C) Lady Russell (*Persuasion*)

3. In Jane Austen's day, who was not allowed to attend funerals?

A) children
B) females
C) servants

4. Which feature of Elizabeth Bennet's does Caroline Bingley tease Mr. Darcy about? (*Pride and Prejudice*)

A) her wit
B) her piano playing
C) her eyes

5. "Though Mansfield Park might have some pains, Portsmouth could have no _____." (Fanny Price)

A) freedom
B) balm
C) pleasures

6. Which Jane Austen novel did Keanu Reeves' and Sandra Bullock's characters discuss in *The Lake House*?

A) *Persuasion*
B) *Sense and Sensibility*
C) *Northanger Abbey*

7. Whom does Catherine Morland suspect of killing his wife in *Northanger Abbey*?

A) General Tilney
B) Mr. Allen
C) Mr. Morland

8. Who says this?
". . .it is always incomprehensible to a man that a woman should ever refuse an offer of marriage. A man always imagines a woman to be ready for anybody who asks her."

A) Elizabeth Bennet (*Pride and Prejudice*)
B) Emma Woodhouse (*Emma*)
C) Lady Russell (*Persuasion*)

9. In Jane Austen's day, men and women ate separately for which meal?

10. Which word could be used to describe Lady Susan? (*Lady Susan*)

A) rich
B) scheming
C) mournful

11. Who says this?
"Mr. Edward Ferrars, it seems, has been engaged above this twelvemonth to my cousin Lucy!" (*Sense and Sensibility*)

A) Mrs. Jennings
B) Eliza Williams
C) Anne Steele

12. Which British pop star played Fanny Price in the 2007 BBC version of *Mansfield Park*?

A) Cheryl Cole
B) Ellie Goulding
C) Billie Piper

13. What is the name of the estate leased to Charles Bingley? (*Pride and Prejudice*)

A) Rosings
B) Longbourn
C) Netherfield Park

14. "There is safety in reserve, but no _____. One cannot love a reserved person." (Frank Churchill, *Emma*)

A) passion
B) attraction
C) spirit

15. In Jane's day, "getting one's hair cut" was slang for
_____.

A) visiting a lady
B) going on a drinking binge
C) discussing an inheritance

16. What does Catherine Morland find in the mysterious cabinet in her room? (*Northanger Abbey*)

A) a secret journal
B) a map of the abbey
C) a laundry list

17. Whom are they discussing?
"The lady then. . .is very rich?"
"Fifty thousand pounds, my dear."

A) Miss Grey (*Sense and Sensibility*)
B) Georgiana Darcy (*Pride and Prejudice*)
C) Emma Woodhouse (*Emma*)

18. What is the title of a rewrite of *Mansfield Park* involving ancient Egyptian curses?

A) *Mummy in Mansfield*
B) *Fanny's Curse*
C) *Mansfield Park and Mummies*

19. What are the names of the tenants who rent Kellynch Hall in *Persuasion*?

A) Charles and Mary Musgrove
B) Admiral and Mrs. Croft
C) Captain and Mrs. Harville

20. Whom does Jane Austen say was raised by "an illiterate and miserly father" to explain his lack of manners?

A) Mr. Wickham (*Pride and Prejudice*)
B) Mr. Collins (*Pride and Prejudice*)
C) Mr. Elliot (*Persuasion*)

21. Who said it?
"I should hardly like to live with [Jane Austen's] ladies and gentlemen, in their elegant but confined houses."

A) George Eliot
B) Elizabeth Gaskell
C) Charlotte Brontë

22. Who secretly gives Jane Fairfax a pianoforte? (*Emma*)

A) Mr. Knightley
B) Frank Churchill
C) Mr. Dixon

23. Who says this?
"All the privilege I claim for my own sex (it is not a very enviable one: you need not covet it), is that of loving longest, when existence or when hope is gone!"

A) Fanny Price (*Mansfield Park*)
B) Elinor Dashwood (*Sense and Sensibility*)
C) Anne Elliot (*Persuasion*)

24. *From Prada to Nada* is a loose film adaptation of which Austen novel?

A) *Sense and Sensibility*
B) *Northanger Abbey*
C) *Emma*

25. What is the name for the collection of stories and plays that Jane wrote before she wrote her first novel?

A) *Juvenilia*
B) *Junior Writings*
C) *Blooms*

26. Whom does this describe?
"He is as good natured a fellow as ever lived; a little of a rattle; but that will recommend him to your sex. . ."

A) Henry Crawford (*Mansfield Park*)
B) John Thorpe (*Northanger Abbey*)
C) George Wickham (*Pride and Prejudice*)

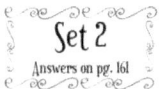

Set 2
Answers on pg. 161

---

27. Where is The Jane Austen Centre located?

A) Bath
B) London
C) Lyme

---

28. What did Mrs. Price regularly lament during Fanny's stay at Portsmouth? (*Mansfield Park*)

A) the streak-marked spoons
B) Fanny's lack of a husband
C) the ragged carpet

---

29. Who says this?
"A woman must have a thorough knowledge of music, singing, drawing, dancing, and the modern languages [to be accomplished]."

A) Elizabeth Elliot (*Persuasion*)
B) Mrs. Elton (*Emma*)
C) Caroline Bingley (*Pride and Prejudice*)

---

30. What is the name of a "monster" version of *Emma* written by Wayne Josephson?

A) *Werewolf Emma*
B) *Emma and the Vampires*
C) *Emma Frankenstein*

31. Which of the following novels was originally written as an epistolary novel, or novel in letters?

A) *Northanger Abbey*
B) *Sense and Sensibility*
C) *Emma*

32. Who says this?
"If there is anything disagreeable going on men are always sure to get out of it."

A) Maria Bertram (*Mansfield Park*)
B) Elizabeth Bennet (*Pride and Prejudice*)
C) Mary Musgrove (*Persuasion*)

33. What is the name of the Austen home where Jane was raised?

A) Southampton Lodge
B) Chawton Cottage
C) Steventon Rectory

34. What is the name of the second estate Henry Tilney often must visit? (*Northanger Abbey*)

A) Woodston
B) Thornton Lacey
C) Allenham

35. Whom does this describe?
"She was a woman who spent her days in sitting, nicely dressed, on a sofa, doing some long piece of needlework, of little use and no beauty, thinking more of her pug than her children…"

A) Lady Bertram (*Mansfield Park*)
B) Mrs. Allen (*Northanger Abbey*)
C) Lady Dalrymple (*Persuasion*)

36. What is the title of a musical movie version of *Pride and Prejudice* set in India? (2004)

37. Which Austen work boasts a heroine named Emma (besides the novel *Emma*)?

A) *Lady Susan*
B) *The Watsons*
C) *Sanditon*

38. Whom does this describe?
"Her own family were plain, matter-of-fact people who seldom aimed a wit of any kind; her father, at the utmost, being contented with a pun, and her mother with a proverb."

A) Lucy Steele's (*Sense and Sensibility*)
B) Fanny Price's (*Mansfield Park*)
C) Catherine Morland's (*Northanger Abbey*)

39. Which event is rumored to have caused Jane Austen to faint?

A) her father's death
B) learning of her upcoming move to Bath
C) her first novel's acceptance

40. Which of the following characters plays the harp?

A) Mary Crawford (*Mansfield Park*)
B) Anne Elliot (*Persuasion*)
C) Eleanor Tilney (*Northanger Abbey*)

41. "Every neighborhood should have a great lady. The great lady of Sanditon was Lady _____." (*Sanditon*)

A) Brereton
B) Parker
C) Denham

42. What is the name of the *Crouching Tiger, Hidden Dragon* director who also directed a Jane Austen adaptation?

43. What did Admiral Croft have removed from Sir Walter Elliot's former bedchamber after the Elliots moved out? (*Persuasion*)

A) an ornate bed
B) several looking glasses
C) an extra wardrobe

44. Who says this?
"I suppose there may be a hundred different ways of being in love."

A) Mary Crawford (*Mansfield Park*)
B) Emma Woodhouse (*Emma*)
C) Elinor Dashwood (*Sense and Sensibility*)

45. Who said it?
"Jane Austen is the pinnacle to which all other authors aspire."

A) A. S. Byatt
B) J. K. Rowling
C) Joan Aiken

46. Who is neighbor and landlord to the Dashwood girls? (*Sense and Sensibility*)

A) Mr. Willoughby
B) Colonel Brandon
C) Sir John Middleton

47. Whom does this describe?
"[For her sister,] she had fixed on Tom Bertram; the eldest son of a Baronet was not too good for a girl of twenty thousand pounds." (*Mansfield Park*)

A) Mrs. Grant
B) Susan Price
C) Mary Crawford

48. Who played Henry Tilney in the 1986 adaptation of *Northanger Abbey*?

A) Timothy Dalton
B) Peter Firth
C) Michael Gambon

49. Finish the sentence:

"It is a truth universally acknowledged, that a single man in possession of a good fortune, must be _____."
(*Pride and Prejudice*)

50. Who says this?
"There is exquisite pleasure in subduing an insolent spirit, in making a person pre-determined to dislike, acknowledge one's superiority."

A) Catherine de Bourgh (*Pride and Prejudice*)
B) Lady Susan (*Lady Susan*)
C) Henry Crawford (*Mansfield Park*)

51. Why was Jane Austen's aunt Jane Leigh-Perrot sent to prison?

A) for stealing some lace
B) for being a Bonapartist
C) for adultery

Set 3
Answers on pg. 163

52. Where in Bath does Lady Dalrymple live? (*Persuasion*)

A) Camden Park
B) Laura Place
C) Westgate Building

53. Who says this to Elizabeth Bennet?
"Here are officers enough in Meryton to disappoint all the young ladies in the country. Let Wickham be your man. He is a pleasant fellow, and would jilt you creditably." (*Pride and Prejudice*)

A) Colonel Forster
B) Mr. Denny
C) Mr. Bennet

54. Who played Fanny Price in the version of *Mansfield Park* released in 1999?

A) Frances O'Connor
B) Embeth Davidtz
C) Victoria Hamilton

55. Who resides at Donwell Abbey? (*Emma*)

A) Emma Woodhouse
B) Mr. Knightley
C) Mr. and Mrs. Elton

56. Whom does this describe?
"Her skin was very brown. . .and in her eyes, which were very dark, there was a life, a spirit, and eagerness which could hardly be seen without delight."

A) Marianne Dashwood (*Sense and Sensibility*)
B) Mary Crawford (*Mansfield Park*)
C) Isabella Thorpe (*Northanger Abbey*)

57. How long would a typical dance at a ball last in Jane Austen's time?

A) 8 minutes
B) 15 minutes
C) 20 minutes

58. How much money would Georgianna Darcy bring into a marriage? (*Pride and Prejudice*)

A) £10,000
B) £20,000
C) £30,000

59. Whom is Isabella Thorpe talking to?
"Oh! that arch eye of yours! - It sees through every thing." (*Northanger Abbey*)

A) John Thorpe
B) Captain Tilney
C) Catherine Morland

60. Whom does Sophie Thompson play in the 1995 film version of *Persuasion*?

A) Louisa Musgrove
B) Mary Musgrove
C) Elizabeth Elliot

61. Which novel opens with an injury in a carriage crash?

A) *Lady Susan*
B) *The Watsons*
C) *Sanditon*

62. Whom does this describe?
"Whatever he said, was said well; and whatever he did, done gracefully."

A) George Wickham (*Pride and Prejudice*)
B) Henry Crawford (*Mansfield Park*)
C) Mr. Willoughby (*Sense and Sensibility*)

63. Who made Jane Austen's clothing?

A) her mother
B) a dressmaker
C) she did

64. What information does Lucy Steele confide to Elinor? (*Sense and Sensibility*)

A) That her sister has eloped.
B) That she is engaged to Edward.
C) That she will inherit a large sum.

65. Whom does this describe?
"Captain Wentworth should be allowed some credit for the self-command with which he attended to her large fat sighings over the destiny of a son, whom alive nobody had cared for." (*Persuasion*)

A) Lady Dalrymple
B) Lady Russell
C) Mrs. Musgrove

66. Which literary great wrote "The Janeites," a short story about WWI soldiers who find escape in Jane Austen's novels?

A) Rudyard Kipling
B) Ernest Hemingway
C) Edith Wharton

67. Which leading man appears to know a lot about muslin?

A) Edmund Bertram (*Mansfield Park*)
B) George Knightley (*Emma*)
C) Henry Tilney (*Northanger Abbey*)

68. Whom does this describe?
". . .his fault, a liking to make girls fall in love with him, is not half so dangerous to a wife's happiness, as a tendency to fall in love himself."

A) Frederick Tilney (*Northanger Abbey*)
B) George Wickham (*Pride and Prejudice*)
C) Henry Crawford (*Mansfield Park*)

69. Who said it?
"All that interests any character introduced [in Austen's novels] is still this one: Has he or she the money to marry with, and conditions, conforming? ... Suicide is more respectable."

A) Samuel Coleridge
B) Henry David Thoreau
C) Ralph Waldo Emerson

70. Where is Kellynch Hall located? (*Persuasion*)

A) Somersetshire
B) Lyme
C) Bath

71. Who says this?
"Oh, dear, yes, I know [Mr. Willoughby] extremely well! Not that I ever spoke to him indeed; but I have seen him for ever in town." (*Sense and Sensibility*)

A) Charlotte Palmer
B) Fanny Dashwood
C) Lady Middleton

72. Which of the following movies is an adaptation of a Jane Austen novel?

A) *The Notebook*
B) *When Harry Met Sally*
C) *Clueless*
D) *North and South*

73. Who invites Lydia Bennet to go to Brighton? (*Pride and Prejudice*)

A) the Hursts
B) the Forsters
C) the Gardiners

74. "The person, be it gentleman or lady, who has not pleasure in a good novel, must be intolerably _____." (Henry Tilney, *Northanger Abbey*)

A) ignorant
B) boring
C) stupid

75. The game of "whist" was often played in Austen's day. How many cards are dealt to each player at the beginning?

A) seven
B) eleven
C) thirteen

76. Who surprises the Dashwood women with a visit at their cottage?
(*Sense and Sensibility*)

A) Edward Ferrars
B) Fanny Dashwood
C) Eliza Williams

Set 4
Answers on pg. 165

77. Who says it?
"My being charming. . .is not quite enough to induce me to marry; I must find other people charming—one other person at least."

A) Emma Woodhouse (*Emma*)
B) Elizabeth Bennet (*Pride and Prejudice*)
C) Marianne Dashwood (*Sense and Sensibility*)

78. In what 2010 re-imagining of *Mansfield Park* is Fanny Price found murdered?

A) *Murder at Mansfield Park*
B) *Mansfield Park Mystery*
C) *Manslaughter Park*

79. Which novel does Catherine Morland read that talked of a black veil?
(*Northanger Abbey*)

A) *The Romance of the Forest*
B) *The Mysteries of Udolpho*
C) *The Monk*

80. Whom does this describe?
"He had been engaged to Captain Harville's sister, and was now mourning her loss. They had been a year or two waiting for fortune and promotion."

A) Mr. Elton (*Sense and Sensibility*)
B) Frederick Tilney (*Northanger Abbey*)
C) Captain James Benwick (*Persuasion*)

81. On which novel did Jane Austen's name finally appear (as opposed to being simply called "A Lady")?

A) *Mansfield Park*
B) *Northanger Abbey*
C) *Emma*

82. What is the name of the suitor that broke Elizabeth Watson's heart? (*The Watsons*)

A) Dr. Harding
B) Mr. Purvis
C) Mr. Howard

83. Whom does this describe?
"Matrimony was her object, provided she could marry well, and having seen Mr. Bertram in town, she knew that objection could no more be made to his person than to his situation in life."

A) Mary Crawford (*Mansfield Park*)
B) Augusta Hawkins (*Emma*)
C) Louisa Musgrove (*Persuasion*)

84. Which character does Billy Nighy play in the 2020 version of *Emma*?

A) Mr. Weston
B) Mr. Elton
C) Mr. Woodhouse

85. Whom is Mrs. Phillips related to? (*Pride and Prejudice*)

86. Who says this?
"Sometimes one is guided by what they say of themselves, and very frequently by what other people say of them, without giving oneself time to deliberate and judge."

A) Anne Elliot (*Persuasion*)
B) Elinor Dashwood (*Sense and Sensibility*)
C) Fanny Price (*Mansfield Park*)

---

87. What did Jane Austen always wear, according to her niece Caroline?

A) a cross necklace
B) a silver ring
C) a cap

---

88. Where does Louisa Musgrove's accident occur? (*Persuasion*)

A) Bath
B) Shropshire
C) Lyme

---

89. "_____ working on a weak head produces every sort of mischief." (Mr. Knightley, *Emma*)

A) Infatuation
B) Vanity
C) Vexation

---

90. What is the name of Stephanie Barron's series of novels that has Jane Austen working as a master sleuth?

A) *Jane Austen's Whodunit*
B) *The Jane Austen Mysteries*
C) *Murder in Jane Austen Country*

91. Which Austen work has a main character who is a blatant adulteress?

A) *Lady Susan*
B) *The Watsons*
C) *Sanditon*

92. Whom does this describe?
"[Her] vacancy of mind and incapacity for thinking were such, that as she never talked a great deal, so she could never be entirely silent. . ."

A) Mrs. Bennet (*Pride and Prejudice*)
B) Mrs. Allen (*Northanger Abbey*)
C) Mrs. Norris (*Mansfield Park*)

93. Who said it?
"Good sense, courage, contentment, fortitude. . . These are the concepts by which Jane Austen grasps the world."

A) J. R. R. Tolkien
B) Martin Amis
C) C.S. Lewis

94. Where does Marianne finally see Willoughby after he left Barton suddenly? (*Sense and Sensibility*)

A) At a large party in London
B) At Mrs. Jenning's estate
C) At Colonel Brandon's picnic

95. Who says this?
"[A woman] must yet add something more substantial, in the improvement of her mind by extensive reading."

A) Mr. Darcy (*Pride and Prejudice*)
B) Henry Tilney (*Northanger Abbey*)
C) Mr. Woodhouse (*Emma*)

96. Which book contains this quote?
"You'll be fascinated to learn (from me that hates novels) that I finally got round to Jane Austen and went out of my mind over *Pride & Prejudice* which I can't bring myself to bring back to the library till you find me a copy of my own."

A) *Letters to Alice: On First Reading Jane Austen*
B) *84, Charing Cross Road*
C) *The Jane Austen Project*

97. When Captain Wentworth visits the Crofts in *Persuasion*, how long had it been since Anne Elliot had broken off their engagement?

A) about six years
B) about eight years
C) about ten years

98. Who says this?
"It is such a happiness when good people get together—and they always do."

A) Mrs. Jennings (*Sense and Sensibility*)
B) Miss Bates (*Emma*)
C) Jane Bennet (*Pride and Prejudice*)

99. Who contributed to *Memoir of Jane Austen* (1870)?

A) Jane's cousins
B) Jane's sister
C) Jane's nieces and nephews

100. Whom does Isabella Thorpe marry? (*Northanger Abbey*)

A) no one
B) James Morland
C) Captain Tilney

101. Whom does this describe?
"It was impossible for her to say what she did not feel, however trivial the occasion; and upon [her] therefore the whole task of telling lies when politeness required it, always fell."

A) Elinor Dashwood (*Sense and Sensibility*)
B) Fanny Price (*Mansfield Park*)
C) Anne Elliot (*Persuasion*)

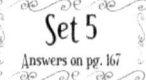

Set 5
Answers on pg. 167

---

102. What is the main character's name in the film *Austenland* (2013)?

A) Jane
B) Elizabeth
C) Emma

---

103. True or false?

Captain Wentworth proposes to Anne Elliot for the second time while they are visiting Lyme. (*Persuasion*)

---

104. Whom does this describe?
"[He] can please where he chuses. He does not want abilities. He can be a conversible companion if he thinks it worth his while."

A) John Thorpe (*Northanger Abbey*)
B) John Willoughby (*Sense and Sensibility*)
C) Mr. Darcy (*Pride and Prejudice*)

---

105. Who was responsible for destroying most of Jane Austen's letters?

A) her mother
B) her sister
C) her nephew

106. What does Marianne Dashwood not believe in? (*Sense and Sensibility*)

A) second attachments
B) love at first sight
C) communicating her feelings

107. Whom does this describe?
"The circumstance of [his] commission as Second Lieutenant of H.M. Sloop Thrush being made out was spreading general joy through a wide circle of great people."

A) Colonel Fitzwilliam (*Pride and Prejudice*)
B) William Price (*Mansfield Park*)
C) James Benwick (*Persuasion*)

108. Who played Catherine Morland in the 2007 film version of *Northanger Abbey?*

A) Carey Mulligan
B) Catherine Walker
C) Felicity Jones

109. Whom does Mrs. Croft describe as "very good humoured, unaffected girls"? (*Persuasion*)

A) the Elliot sisters
B) the Musgrove sisters
C) the Dalrymples

110. Who says this?
"But it is never safe to sit out of doors my dear."

A) Mrs. Norris (*Mansfield Park*)
B) Mr. Woodhouse (*Emma*)
C) Mrs. Bennet (*Pride and Prejudice*)

111. Which disease probably took Jane Austen's life?

A) Lou Gehrig's Disease
B) Addison's Disease
C) Parkinson's Disease

112. Who is Lady Denham's companion? (*Sanditon*)

A) Clara Brereton
B) Susan Parker
C) Miss Beaufort

113. Whom does this describe?
"[They felt] that, in forcing [Catherine] on such a measure,
General Tilney had acted neither honourably nor feelingly –
neither as a gentleman nor as a parent." (*Northanger Abbey*)

A) Mr. and Mrs. Thorpe
B) Mr. and Mrs. Allen
C) Mr. and Mrs. Morland

114. A.A. Milne, author of *Winnie the Pooh*, adapted which
of Jane Austen's novels for the stage in 1936?

115. Which *Sense and Sensibility* character is running for a
seat in Parliament?

A) Colonel Brandon
B) Robert Ferrars
C) Thomas Palmer

116. Who says this?
". . .there is not one in a hundred of either sex who is not taken in when they marry."

A) Emma Woodhouse (*Emma*)
B) Charlotte Lucas (*Pride and Prejudice*)
C) Mary Crawford (*Mansfield Park*)

117. Who said it?
"Jane [Austen] is entirely impossible. It seems a great pity that they allowed her to die a natural death."

A) Elizabeth Barrett Browning
B) Mark Twain
C) H. W. Garrod

118. Whom does the group of walkers meet on the way back to the cottage in *Persuasion*?

A) the Crofts
B) the Elliots
C) the Dalrymples

119. Whom is Mr. Bennet talking to Mrs. Bennet about?
". . . if your daughter should have a dangerous fit of illness, if she should die, it would be a comfort to know that it was all in pursuit of [him]."
(*Pride and Prejudice*)

A) Mr. Bingley
B) Mr. Darcy
C) Mr. Wickham

120. What is *Jane Austen Unbound*?

A) a literary conference
B) an online game
C) a collection of Austen's letters

121. What does John Thorpe generally talk about?
(*Northanger Abbey*)

A) carriages
B) card games
C) hunting

122. Whom does this describe?
"She was a very pretty girl. . . She was short, plump and fair, with a fine bloom, blue eyes, light hair, regular features, and a look of great sweetness."

A) Harriet Smith (*Emma*)
B) Marianne Dashwood (*Sense and Sensibility*)
C) Louisa Musgrove (*Persuasion*)

123. Which heroine did Jane Austen's mother call "insipid"?

A) Mary Bennet
B) Lady Susan
C) Fanny Price

124. Who elopes with Julia Bertram? (*Mansfield Park*)

A) William Price
B) Dr. Grant
C) John Yates

125. Whom does this describe?
"Elinor soon allowed them credit for some kind of sense . . ."
(*Sense and Sensibility*)

A) the Palmers
B) the Miss Steeles
C) the Mortons

126. In the movie *Lost in Austen,* whom does Jane Bennet marry?

A) Mr. Wickham
B) Mr. Collins
C) Mr. Darcy

Set 6
Answers on pg. 169

127. True or false?

When *Persuasion* begins, the Napoleonic wars have just begun.

128. Who says this?
"We have all a better guide in ourselves, if we would attend to it, than any other person can be."

A) Anne Elliot (*Persuasion*)
B) Fanny Price (*Mansfield Park*)
C) Charlotte Lucas (*Pride and Prejudice*)

129. Why were books particularly expensive until 1861?

A) Because so few people were literate.
B) Because of the man power it took to print books.
C) Because of a heavy tax on paper.

130. Why is Mrs. Dashwood unwilling to leave Norland so soon? (*Sense and Sensibility*)

A) She grew up there.
B) Elinor is developing an attachment for Edward.
C) She and her family have nowhere to go.

131. Who says this?
"I have more than once repented that I did not marry [Sir James Martin] myself; and were he but one degree less contemptibly weak I certainly should."

A) Lady Susan Vernon (*Lady Susan*)
B) Miss Esther Denham (*Sanditon*)
C) Emma Watson (*The Watsons*)

132. Which of the following, published in 1913, was the first "sequel" to *Pride and Prejudice*?

A) *Old Friends and New Fancies*
B) *Pemberley*
C) *Promise and Perseverence*

133. Whose lies lead General Tilney to believe Catherine Morland is an heiress? (*Northanger Abbey*)

A) John Thorpe's
B) Captain Tilney's
C) Mr. Allen's

134. Whom is being described?
"[She has] the power of having rather too much her own way. and a disposition to think a little too well of herself."

A) Marianne Dashwood (*Sense and Sensibility*)
B) Maria Bertram (*Mansfield Park*)
C) Emma Woodhouse (*Emma*)

135. Why was Jane Austen's brother James' last name changed to Knight?

A) He had a row with his father.
B) He was adopted by another family.
C) He prefered a more dignified-sounding name.

136. What event led to Fanny Price's consequence increasing at Mansfield Park?

A) her "coming out"
B) Maria's marriage and departure with Julia
C) Mr. Crawford's proposal of marriage

137. Whom does this describe?
"They were in love with him; yet there it was not love. It was a little fever of admiration . . . "

A) the Miss Steeles (*Sense and Sensibility*)
B) the Miss Musgroves (*Persuasion*)
C) the Miss Bertrams (*Mansfield Park*)

138. In which "monster" version of *Pride and Prejudice* is Elizabeth Bennet a master ninja?

139. What was Harriet Smith's most valuable "treasure," kept to remember Mr. Elton? (*Emma*)

A) the end of an old pencil
B) a handkerchief
C) a court plaster

140. Catherine Morland's father was described as "a very respectable man, though his name was _____."
(*Northanger Abbey*)

A) Richard
B) Bartholomew
C) Fitzwilliam

141. Who said it?
"I am a Janeite, and therefore slightly imbecile about Jane
Austen. . . She is my favourite author! I read and re-read,
the mouth open and the mind closed."

A) Graham Greene
B) Upton Sinclair
C) E. M. Forster

142. What is Captain Wentworth's brother's profession?
(*Persuasion*)

A) shopkeeper
B) curate
C) sailor

143. Whom is Mr. Bingley talking to?

"I must have you dance. I hate to see you standing about by
yourself in this stupid manner. You had much better
dance." (*Pride and Prejudice*)

144. Which actress was originally hired to play Marianne
Dashwood in *Sense and Sensibility* (1995) before Kate
Winslet stepped in?

A) Kate Beckinsale
B) Amanda Root
C) Sophie Thompson

145. Which other character is Fanny thinking of? (*Mansfield
Park*)
"They were two solitary sufferers, or connected only by
Fanny's consciousness."

A) Maria Bertram
B) Mary Crawford
C) Julia Bertram

146. "A lady, without a family, was the very best
_____ in the world." (*Persuasion*)

A) expert on love
B) preserver of furniture
C) companion

147. True or false?

Jane Austen's works have never been out of print.

148. What does General Tilney mention is growing in his
greenhouses? (*Northanger Abbey*)

A) melons
B) pineapples
C) mangoes

149. Whom does this describe?
"It was contrary to every doctrine of hers that difference of fortune
should keep any couple asunder who were attracted by resemblance of
disposition."

A) Mrs. Dashwood (*Sense and Sensibility*)
B) Lady Russell (*Persuasion*)
C) Mrs. Allen (*Northanger Abbey*)

150. *Eligible* (2016) by Curtis Sittenfield is an adaptation of which
Austen novel?

A) *Sense and Sensibility*
B) *Emma*
C) *Pride and Prejudice*

151. "A private dance without _____ was pronounced an infamous fraud upon the rights of men and women." (*Emma*)

A) a good number of gentlemen
B) a waltz
C) sitting down to supper

152. What does Henry Tilney compare a country dance to? (*Northanger Abbey*)

A) dressmaking
B) marriage
C) horse riding

153. How was Reverand Thomas Fowle connected to Jane Austen?

A) He was her sister's fiancé.
B) He was her pastor.
C) He was her cousin.

154. Which activity takes place at the Elliot's evening party? (*Persuasion*)

A) dancing
B) card playing
C) opera

155. Whom does this describe?

"[She] has no discretion in her coughs," said her father; "she times them ill."

A) Kitty Bennet (*Pride and Prejudice*)
B) Emma Woodhouse (*Emma*)
C) Anne Elliot (*Persuasion*)

156. Cloris Leachman played which character in a live television version of *Sense and Sensibility* in 1950?

A) Elinor Dashwood
B) Marianne Dashwood
C) Fanny Dashwood

157. In each of Austen's main novels (except *Northanger Abbey*), a major event occurs on which day of the week?

A) Tuesday
B) Friday
C) Sunday

158. Whom is being described?
"She does not confine herself to that sort of honest flirtation which satisfies most people, but aspires to the more delicious gratification of making a whole family miserable."

A) Isabella Thorpe (*Northanger Abbey*)
B) Susan Vernon (*Lady Susan*)
C) Lydia Bennet (*Pride and Prejudice*)

159. Who sent out invitations to balls three to six weeks in advance?

A) the lady of the house
B) the father figure of the house
C) the eldest daughter

160. Where does John Thorpe take Catherine in his carriage? (*Northanger Abbey*)

A) To Northanger Abbey
B) To Fullterton
C) To Claverton Down

161. "There are certainly not so many men of _____ in the world, as there are pretty women to deserve them." (*Mansfield Park*)

A) large fortune
B) good manners
C) intelligence

162. Which "sequel" to *Mansfield Park* was completed by Jane's great grand-niece in 1930?

A) *Mansfield Park Legacy*
B) *Edmund and Fanny*
C) *Susan Price, or Resolution*

163. What is most likely Mrs. Bennet's first name? (*Pride and Prejudice*)

A) Elizabeth
B) Mary
C) Jane

164. Who says this?
"I declare after all there is no enjoyment like reading! How much sooner one tires of any thing than of a book!" (*Pride and Prejudice*)

A) Mary Bennet
B) Caroline Bingley
C) Elizabeth Bennet

165. What is the term George Saintsbury coined to describe a Jane Austen enthusiast?

166. Lucy Steele refers to her sister as "Nancy," a nickname for her real name, which is _____. (*Sense and Sensibility*)

A) Naomi
B) Anne
C) Anastasia

167. Who says this?
"Mrs. Clay has been using [Gowland's lotion] at my recommendation, and you see what it has done for her. You see how it has carried away her freckles." (*Persuasion*)

A) Elizabeth Elliot
B) Sir Walter Elliot
C) Mrs. Croft

168. Who played Mr. Knightley in the 1996 version of *Emma* starring Kate Beckinsale?

A) Jeremy Northam
B) Jonny Lee Miller
C) Mark Strong

169. "Woman is fine for her own satisfaction alone. No man will admire her the more, no woman will _____ her the better for it." (*Northanger Abbey*)

A) like
B) despise
C) respect

170. Whom does this describe?
"[She] could never love by halves; and her whole heart became, in time, as much devoted to her husband as it had once been to [another man]."

A) Harriet Smith (*Emma*)
B) Marianne Dashwood (*Sense and Sensibility*)
C) Louisa Musgrove (*Persuasion*)

171. What is Michaelmas—a common holiday reference in Jane Austen's novels?

172. Why doesn't Mr. Bingley visit Jane in London? (*Pride and Prejudice*)

A) Mr. Darcy convinced him not to.
B) He was unaware she was there.
C) He was too busy seeing Georgiana.

173. Who says this?
"I could not have visited Mrs. Robert Martin, of Abbey-Mill Farm."
(*Emma*)

A) Mr. Elton
B) Harriet Smith
C) Emma Woodhouse

174. Jane Austen's niece, Catherine Hubback, completed which novel (which she entitled *The Younger Sister*)?

A) *Sanditon*
B) *Lady Susan*
C) *The Watsons*

175. Whose estate is most likely funded by slave labor?

A) Thomas Bertram's (*Mansfield Park*)
B) Colonel Brandon's (*Sense and Sensibility*)
C) General Tilney's (*Northanger Abbey*)

176. Whom does this describe?
"Few women could think more of their personal appearance than he did, nor would the valet of any new made lord be more delighted with the place he held in society."

A) Henry Crawford (*Mansfield Park*)
B) Sir Walter Elliot (*Persuasion*)
C) Frank Churchill (*Emma*)

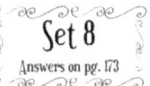

Set 8

Answers on pg. 173

177. Which Cheshire home was the inspiration for Pemberley?

A) Lyme Park
B) Chatsworth
C) Longleat

178. How much per annum were James and Isabella promised when they marry? (*Northanger Abbey*)

A) £200
B) £400
C) £600

179. Who says this?
"In matters of greater weight, I may suffer from want of money. Younger sons cannot marry where they like." (*Pride and Prejudice*)

A) Colonel Fitzwilliam
B) Mr. Bingley
C) Mr. Wickham

180. Who played Emma in the movie adaptation of the same name in 1972?

A) Doran Godwin
B) Ann Firbank
C) Elizabeth Garvie

181. To which city do the Allens take Catherine in *Northanger Abbey*?

A) Brighton
B) Bath
C) London

182. Whom does this describe?

"[Her] first glance told her that Sir Edward's air was that of a lover. There could be no doubt of his devotion to Clara."

A) Emma Watson (*The Watsons*)
B) Charlotte Heywood (*Sanditon*)
C) Lady Susan Vernon (*Lady Susan*)

183. True or false?

In Jane Austen's day, tea taxes were sometimes over 100%.

184. Who believes that nursing is a woman's job? (*Persuasion*)

A) Mary Musgrove
B) Charles Musgrove
C) Anne Elliot

185. In which Austen work does this appear?
"I cannot say much for [Henry the 6th's] Sense–Nor would I if I could, for he was a Lancastrian. I suppose you know all about the Wars between him and the Duke of York who was of the right side."

A) *The History of England*
B) *Love and Freindship*
C) *The Watsons*

186. Whom was Emma Thompson speaking of (with regards to her film *Sense and Sensibility*)?

"Why did we cast him? He's much prettier than I am."

187. Which novel was originally titled *First Impressions*?

A) *Sense and Sensibility*
B) *Northanger Abbey*
C) *Pride and Prejudice*

188. Whom does this describe?
"If this man had not twelve thousand a year, he would be a very stupid fellow."

A) Mr. Rushworth (*Mansfield Park*)
B) Charles Musgrove (*Persuasion*)
C) John Willoughby (*Sense and Sensibility*)

189. Who said it?
"What a pity such a gifted creature died so early."

A) Robert Burns
B) Emily Brontë
C) Sir Walter Scott

190. Why does Captain Tilney suddenly want Catherine to leave his house? (*Northanger Abbey*)

A) She entered his wife's room.
B) She stole a novel from their shelves.
C) He discovered she's not rich.

191. Who says this?

"Good company requires only birth, education and manners, and with regard to education is not very nice." (*Persuasion*)

A) Mr. Elliot
B) Sir Walter Elliot
C) Admiral Croft

192. Which Hollywood legend was kicked out of her childhood home when she refused to give up her stage role as Elizabeth Bennet?

A) Barbara Stanwyck
B) Olivia de Havilland
C) Deborah Kerr

193. How is Mr. Knightley "related," or connected, to Emma Woodhouse? (*Emma*)

194. Who says this?

"I am sure of this—that if everybody was to drink their bottle a-day, there would not be half the disorders in the world there are now."

A) John Thorpe (*Northanger Abbey*)
B) Frank Churchill (*Emma*)
C) William Elliot (*Persuasion*)

195. Who was not socially permitted to leave his/her own calling card at somebody's house?

A) an unmarried girl
B) a suitor
C) a peddler

196. Whom does Frederica marry? (*Lady Susan*)

A) Sir James Martin
B) Mr. Manwaring
C) Reginald de Courcy

197. Who says this?
"Oh! Single, my dear, to be sure! A single man of large fortune; four or five thousand a year. What a fine thing for our girls!"

A) Lady Bertram (*Mansfield Park*)
B) Mrs. Dashwood (*Sense and Sensibility*)
C) Mrs. Bennet (*Pride and Prejudice*)

198. Which Downton Abbey actor played Mr. Rushworth in a movie adaptation of *Mansfield Park*?

A) Brendan Coyle
B) Hugh Bonneville
C) Rob James-Collier

199. Who has a duel with Mr. Willoughby? (*Sense and Sensibility*)

A) Colonel Brandon
B) Edward Ferrars
C) Sir John Middleton

200. "There is so little real _____ in the world."
(Mrs. Smith, *Persuasion*)

A) love
B) gossip
C) friendship

201. Who is the only man confirmed to have proposed to Jane Austen?

A) Tom Lefroy
B) Edward Bridges
C) Harris Bigg-Wither

---

202. Who takes Elizabeth Bennet to visit Pemberley the first time? (*Pride and Prejudice*)

A) the Gardiners
B) Mr. Darcy
C) her parents

---

203. Who says this to Catherine Morland?
"When you have finished Udolpho, we will read the Italian together." (*Northanger Abbey*)

A) Isabella Thorpe
B) Henry Tilney
C) Mrs. Allen

---

204. In 2015, Alex Goodwin adapted *Pride and Prejudice* into a picture book using which adorable animals?

A) guinea pigs
B) baby otters
C) kittens

---

205. What is Mr. Elton's first name? (*Emma*)

A) Phineas
B) Philip
C) Richard

206. Who says this?

"The charm is broken. My eyes are opened."

A) Catherine Morland (*Northanger Abbey*)
B) Edmund Bertram (*Mansfield Park*)
C) Elizabeth Bennet (*Pride and Prejudice*)

207. Why was Jane's brother George sent to live with another family?

A) He was adopted out.
B) He was mentally disabled.
C) He was involved in criminal activity.

208. Which Watson child talks mostly of settling bills and arranging money? (*The Watsons*)

A) Robert Watson
B) Sam Watson
C) Penelope Watson

209. Whom is Maria Lucas talking about?

"She is quite a little creature. Who would have thought she could be so thin and small!" (*Pride and Prejudice*)

A) Mrs. Forster
B) Georgiana Darcy
C) Anne de Bourgh

210. BabyLit *TM* used which Austen novel to teach opposites to toddlers?

A) *Sense and Sensibility*
B) *Pride and Prejudice*
C) *Emma*

211. True or false?

Mr. Elliot is a wealthy man when he meets Anne in Lyme.
(*Persuasion*)

212. Whom does this describe?
"She had a thin awkward figure, a sallow skin without colour, dark lank hair, and strong features."

A) Catherine Morland (*Northanger Abbey*)
B) Elinor Dashwood (*Sense and Sensibility*)
C) Fanny Price (*Mansfield Park*)

213. "Miss Austen has no _____. ... What vile creatures her parsons are!" (Cardinal Newman, 1837)

A) imagination
B) romance
C) esteem

214. Where is Sir Thomas Bertram's second estate?
(*Mansfield Park*)

A) Antigua
B) Morocco
C) the East Indies

215. Whom does this describe?
"[She] did not at all approve of what her husband intended to do for his sisters. To take three thousand pounds from the fortune of their dear little boy would be impoverishing him to the most dreadful degree."

A) Lady Bertram (*Mansfield Park*)
B) Fanny Dashwood (*Sense and Sensibility*)
C) Mrs. Gardiner (*Pride and Prejudice*)

216. Which Jane Austen novel does James Stewart's character, Elwood, read to the invisible rabbit in the film *Harvey* (1950)?

A) *Sense and Sensibility*
B) *Emma*
C) *Pride and Prejudice*

217. Where is Longbourn located? (*Pride and Prejudice*)

A) Derbyshire
B) Hertfordshire
C) Kent

218. Whom does this describe?

"She had never boasted either beauty or cleverness. . . The simplicity and cheerfulness of her nature, her contented and grateful spirit, were a recommendation to everybody and a mine of felicity to herself."

A) Henrietta Musgrove (*Persuasion*)
B) Catherine Morland (*Northanger Abbey*)
C) Miss Bates (*Emma*)

219. What was Jane Austen's father's profession?

220. What did "a young man" (Robert Ferrars) debate about for a quarter of an hour while the Miss Dashwoods waited in line at Gray's? (*Sense and Sensibility*)

A) a toothpick case
B) a cigar box
C) a picture frame

221. Whom is Emma talking about?
"I have no doubt that he will thrive and be a very rich man in time–
and his being illiterate and coarse need not disturb us." (*Emma*)

A) Robert Martin
B) Mr. Elton
C) Frank Churchill

222. Which hunk played Captain Wentworth in the 2007 BBC
version of *Persuasion*?

A) Dan Stevens
B) JJ Feild
C) Rupert Penry-Jones

223. "_____ is certainly the finest balm for the pangs of
disappointed love." (*Northanger Abbey*)

A) Reading
B) Travel
C) Friendship

224. Whom does this describe?
"His mother wished to interest him in political concerns, to get him into
parliament, or to see him connected with some of the great men of the
day."

A) Frank Churchill (*Emma*)
B) Edward Ferrars (*Sense and Sensibility*)
C) Edmund Bertram (*Mansfield Park*)

225. True or false?

In Jane's time, a gentleman would only smoke in front of a lady with
her permission.

226. Where does Frank Churchill meet Jane Fairfax? (*Emma*)

A) Bath
B) Weymouth
C) Highbury

Set 10

Answers on pg. 177

227. Whom does this describe?
"[She], at seven and twenty, thought very differently from what
she had been made to think at nineteen."

A) Anne Elliot (*Persuasion*)
B) Charlotte Lucas (*Pride and Prejudice*)
C) Elinor Dashwood (*Sense and Sensibility*)

228. *Jane Austen's Charlotte* (Julia Barrett, 2000) is a completion
of which Austen novel?

A) *Sanditon*
B) *The Watsons*
C) *Lady Susan*

229. Where does Fanny Price's family live? (*Mansfield Park*)

A) Portsmouth
B) Plymouth
C) Preston

230. Whom does this describe?
"With a book he was regardless of time . . ."

A) Henry Tilney (*Northanger Abbey*)
B) Sir Thomas Bertram (*Mansfield Park*)
C) Mr. Bennet (*Pride and Prejudice*)

231. True or false?

Unless a couple were engaged or otherwise "serious" about each other, they could only dance together once at a ball.

232. What part of the body does Louisa Musgrove injure? (*Persuasion*)

A) her leg
B) her head
C) her spine

233. Who says this?
"My Elinor, you do not yet know all my happiness. Colonel Brandon loves Marianne. He has told me so himself." (*Sense and Sensibility*)

A) Charlotte Palmer
B) Mrs. Dashwood
C) Mrs. Jennings

234. Which updated version of *Emma* has Emma as a PR manager and Mr. Knightley the former member of a boy band?

A) *Emma Ever After*
B) *The Emma Diaries*
C) *Emma's Song*

235. What is Mrs. Clay's first name? (*Persuasion*)

A) Penelope
B) Patricia
C) Priscilla

236. Whom does this describe?
"No one who had ever seen [her] in her infancy, would have supposed her born to be an heroine."

A) Catherine Morland (*Northanger Abbey*)
B) Elinor Dashwood (*Sense and Sensibility*)
C) Fanny Price (*Mansfield Park*)

237. Who said it?
"If there is a heaven, Jane Austen is sitting in a small room with Mother Teresa and Princess Diana, listening to Duran Duran, forever. If there's a hell, she's standing."

A) Ricky Gervais
B) Roddy Doyle
C) Eddie Izzard

238. Why do Elizabeth and the Gardiners abandon their vacation early? (*Pride and Prejudice*)

A) Lydia elopes with Mr. Wickham.
B) Mr. Darcy wants them to meet his sister.
C) Lady Catherine will soon visit Longbourn.

239. Whom does this describe?
"He was very much disposed to think Miss Taylor had done as sad a thing for herself as for them, and would have been a great deal happier if she had spent all the rest of her life at Hartfield." (*Emma*)

A) Mr. Weston
B) Mr. Knightley
C) Mr. Woodhouse

240. Who played Marianne Dashwood in the 2008 BBC version of *Sense and Sensibility*?

A) Hattie Morahan
B) Charity Wakefield
C) Lucy Boynton

241. How many children do the Watsons have? (*The Watsons*)

A) four
B) five
C) six

242. Who says this?
"Give a girl an education, and introduce her properly into the world, and ten to one but she has the means of settling well, without farther expense to anybody."

A) Jane Fairfax (*Emma*)
B) Isabella Thorpe (*Northanger Abbey*)
C) Mrs. Norris (*Mansfield Park*)

243. Jane's niece Caroline wrote a memoir entitled _____.

A) *My Aunt Jane Austen*
B) *Jane Austen: A Life*
C) *Becoming Jane*

244. Who is injured and requires nursing, allowing Anne to stay home from a dinner? (*Persuasion*)

A) Anne's sister
B) Anne's cousin
C) Anne's nephew

245. Whom does this describe?
"[She] has deserted my brother, and is to marry yours! Could you have believed there had been such inconstancy and fickleness, and everything that is bad in the world?"

A) Isabella Thorpe (*Northanger Abbey*)
B) Louisa Musgrove (*Persuasion*)
C) Lucy Steele (*Sense and Sensibility*)

246. What is the title of a 2016 novel by Beau North where Mr. Darcy lives the same day over and over?

A) *Mr. Darcy's Groundhog Day*
B) *The Many Lives of Fitzwilliam Darcy*
C) *Elizabeth Improves Upon Acquaintance*

247. Who are Mr. Perry and Mr. Wingfield? (*Emma*)

A) members of the local clergy
B) apothecaries
C) book sellers

248. "One does not love a place the less for _____."
(Anne Elliot, *Persuasion*)

A) its beauty
B) losing a loved one there
C) having suffered in it

249. How many of Jane Austen's brothers were in the Royal Navy?

A) two
B) three
C) four

250. What is Fanny Price's father's profession?
(*Mansfield Park*)

A) sailor
B) shop owner
C) fisherman

251. Who says this?
"A person may be proud without being vain. Pride relates more to our opinion of ourselves, vanity to what we would have others think of us." (*Pride and Prejudice*)

A) Mary Bennet
B) Mrs. Hurst
C) Mr. Darcy

---

252. Which crime writer rewrote *Northanger Abbey*?

A) Susan Hill
B) Frances Hegarty
C) Val McDermid

---

253. Which is true of Colonel Brandon's first love? (*Sense and Sensibility*)

A) She married his brother.
B) She killed herself.
C) She became an actress.

---

254. Whom is being described?
"His two-and-forty speeches! Nobody can ever forget them. Poor fellow!"

A) Mr. Rushworth (*Mansfield Park*)
B) James Benwick (*Persuasion*)
C) Mr. Collins (*Pride and Prejudice*)

---

255. Approximately how many years did Cassandra Austen (Jane's sister) live after Jane's death?

A) 10
B) 20
C) 30

---

256. Who first voices suspicions that Frank Churchill and Jane Fairfax are secretly involved? (*Emma*)

A) Mrs. Weston
B) Harriet Smith
C) Mr. Knightley

257. Which family does this describe?
"The chaise of a traveller being a rare sight in Fullerton, the whole family were immediately at the window." (*Northanger Abbey*)

A) the Thorpes
B) the Morlands
C) the Tilneys

258. Who played Anne Elliot in the 2007 BBC version of *Persuasion*?

A) Sally Hawkins
B) Frances O'Connor
C) Felicity Jones

259. After Mr. Darcy's father dies, how much does Mr. Darcy give to Mr. Wickham so he can study law? (*Pride and Prejudice*)

A) £1000
B) £3000
C) £5000

260. Who says this?
"Business, you know, may bring money, but friendship hardly ever does."

A) Mr. Knightley (*Emma*)
B) Mr. Darcy (*Pride and Prejudice*)
C) Captain Wentworth (*Persuasion*)

261. Who said it?
"All I want to be is the Jane Austen of south Alabama."

A) Zelda Fitzgerald
B) Harper Lee
C) Zora Neale Hurston

262. What had John Dashwood initially "meditated within himself to increase the fortunes of his sisters by"?

A) £100 a year to their mother during her life
B) £1000 apiece
C) £500 apiece

263. Whom is Anne Elliot talking to?
"If I was wrong in yielding to persuasion once, remember that it was to persuasion exerted on the side of safety, not of risk. When I yielded, I thought it was to duty." (*Persuasion*)

A) Captain Benwick
B) Captain Harville
C) Captain Wentworth

264. What is the title of a 2008 "sequel" to *Mansfield Park* in which Mr. and Mrs. Darcy visit the estate to solve a mystery?

A) *The Matters at Mansfield*
B) *Love and Murder*
C) *The Puzzle at Mansfield Park*

265. What is Fanny Price's youngest sister's name? (*Mansfield Park*)

A) Betsey
B) Mary
C) Susan

266. Whom does this describe?
"Music seems scarcely to attract him, and though he admires [her] drawings very much, it is not the admiration of a person who can understand their worth."

A) Mr. Elton (*Emma*)
B) Mr. Darcy (*Pride and Prejudice*)
C) Edward Ferrars (*Sense and Sensibility*)

267. What is a "palisse"?

A) a type of purse
B) a coat dress
C) a style of hat

268. Who died before Captain Benwick could marry her? (*Persuasion*)

A) Miss Cartaret
B) Louisa Musgrove
C) Fanny Harville

269. Whom does this describe?
"Nobody knew better how to dictate liberality to others: but her love of money was equal to her love of directing."

A) Lucy Steele (*Sense and Sensibility*)
B) Mrs. Norris (*Mansfield Park*)
C) Caroline Bingley (*Pride and Prejudice*)

270. Which Jane Austen novel was Meg Ryan's character holding at a café in *You've Got Mail*?

271. Which of the following characters has the greatest income?

A) Mr. Darcy (*Pride and Prejudice*)
B) Mr. Rushworth (*Mansfield Park*)
C) Mr. Knightley (*Emma*)

272. Who says this?
"I do not think any young woman has a right to make a choice that may be disagreeable and inconvenient to the principal part of her family, and be giving bad connections to those who have not been used to them."

A) Mary Musgrove (*Persuasion*)
B) Catherine de Bourgh (*Pride and Prejudice*)
C) Mr. Elton (*Emma*)

273. Jane Austen was the one in her household entrusted with a key to the cabinet holding which commodity?

A) cheese
B) tobacco
C) tea

274. Where does Catherine Morland first meet Henry Tilney? (*Northanger Abbey*)

A) at Northanger Abbey
B) in the Lower Rooms
C) at Mr. Allen's estate

275. Whom does this describe?
"Though little more than sixteen, her figure was formed, and her appearance womanly and graceful. She was less handsome than her brother. . ."

A) Julia Bertram (*Mansfield Park*)
B) Isabella Thorpe (*Northanger Abbey*)
C) Georgiana Darcy (*Pride and Prejudice*)

276. Who played Mr. Knightley in the 2009 mini-series of *Emma*?

A) Jonny Lee Miller
B) Aidan Turner
C) Martin Freeman

Set 12

Answers on pg. 181

---

277. What is Lady Susan's daughter's name? (*Lady Susan*)

A) Catherine
B) Frederica
C) Alicia

---

278. Who says this?
"The mere habit of learning to love is the thing; and a teachableness of disposition in a young lady is a great blessing."

A) Colonel Brandon (*Sense and Sensibility*)
B) Henry Tilney (*Northanger Abbey*)
C) Edmund Bertram (*Mansfield Park*)

---

279. What does the acronym JASNA stand for?

---

280. Which place does Fanny Price refer to as "the Island," prompting her cousins to call her "ignorant"? (*Mansfield Park*)

A) the Isle of Wight
B) Ireland
C) the Isle of Man

281. Whom is Emma talking about?
"Where little minds belong to rich people in authority, I think they have a knack of swelling out, till they are quite as unmanageable as great ones." (*Emma*)

A) the Bateses
B) the Eltons
C) the Churchills

282. Which song does Kate Winslet sing in the 1995 film of *Sense and Sensibility*?

A) "Weep You No More Sad Fountains"
B) "Let the Piano's Martial Blast"
C) "The Meeting of the Waters"

283. At the beginning of *Persuasion*, how long have Admiral and Mrs. Croft been married?

A) 10 years
B) 15 years
C) 20 years

284. Whom is being described?
"Her heart and her judgment were equally against Edmund's decision: she could not acquit his unsteadiness, and his happiness under it made her wretched."

A) Emma Woodhouse (*Emma*)
B) Elinor Dashwood (*Sense and Sensibility*)
C) Fanny Price (*Mansfield Park*)

285. Who said it?
"There are twenty-five elderly gentlemen living in the neighbourhood of London who resent any slight upon [Jane Austen's] genius as if it were an insult to the chastity of their aunts."

A) Flannery O'Connor
B) Virginia Woolf
C) Eudora Welty

286. Why do Henry and Eleanor believe it's impossible their brother is engaged to Isabella? (*Northanger Abbey*)

A) She is already engaged.
B) She is too plain and dull.
C) She is not wealthy enough to consider.

287. Whom does this describe?
"Benevolent, philanthropic man! It was painful to him even to keep a third cousin to himself."

A) Mr. Gardiner (*Pride and Prejudice*)
B) Sir John Middleton (*Sense and Sensibility*)
C) Dr. Grant (*Mansfield Park*)

288. What is the name of a modernized mini-webseries adaptation of *Sanditon* set in California?

A) *Welcome to Sanditon*
B) *Sanditon Beach*
C) *Gigi in Sanditon*

289. Which event in *Pride and Prejudice* was NOT revealed in a letter?

A) Lydia's elopement
B) Wickham's deception
C) Darcy's declaration of love

290. Who says this?
"It is very difficult for the prosperous to be humble."

A) Frank Churchill (*Emma*)
B) Mr. Bingley (*Pride and Prejudice*)
C) Edmund Bertrum (*Mansfield Park*)

291. Jane Austen admitted that one of her suitors had only "one fault. . . It is that his morning coat is a great deal too light." Whom was she talking about?

A) Harris Bigg-Wither
B) Tom Lefroy
C) an "unnamed gentleman"

292. Why did the young people of Mansfield Park travel to Sotherton one summer day?

A) to prepare for a wedding
B) to see the great house and have a picnic
C) to survey the grounds and decide on improvements

293. Whom does this describe?
"[This man's] profession was all that could ever make her friends wish that tenderness less; the dread of a future war all that could dim her sunshine."

A) Colonel Brandon (*Sense and Sensibility*)
B) Mr. Wickham (*Pride and Prejudice*)
C) Frederick Wentworth (*Persuasion*)

294. Who played Catherine Morland in the 1987 TV version of *Northanger Abbey*?

A) Katherine Schlesinger
B) Michelle Arthur
C) Ingrid Lacey

295. What is John Dashwood's son's name?
(*Sense and Sensibility*)

A) Robert
B) Henry
C) Harry

296. Who says this?
"Nothing ever fatigues me but doing what I do not like."

A) Mary Musgrove (*Persuasion*)
B) Mary Crawford (*Mansfield Park*)
C) Mrs. Elton (*Emma*)

297. In Jane Austen's day, traditionally the two official witnesses of a wedding were _____.

A) the fathers of the bride and groom
B) not yet married
C) siblings of the couple

298. Where does everyone initially assume Lydia and Wickham have gone when they elope? (*Pride and Prejudice*)

A) Scotland
B) London
C) Meryton

299. Whom does this describe?
"She was always anxious to get a good husband for every pretty girl."

A) Mrs. Weston (*Emma*)
B) Mrs. Jennings (*Sense and Sensibility*)
C) Mrs. Norris (*Mansfield Park*)

300. Samuel West played _____ in the 1995 version of *Persuasion*.

A) Captain Wentworth
B) Mr. Elliot
C) Charles Musgrove

301. Who operates the school Harriet Smith attended? (*Emma*)

A) Mrs. Hodges
B) Miss Nash
C) Mrs. Goddard

Set 13
Answers on pg. 183

302. Who says this?

"I could easily forgive his pride, if he had not mortified mine."

303. Who wrote a letter to a publishing company in an attempt to get an early version of *Pride and Prejudice* published?

A) Jane's father
B) Jane's brother Frank
C) Jane's sister

304. Whom are Henry and Mary Crawford related to? (*Mansfield Park*)

A) John Yates
B) Mr. Rushworth
C) the local minister's wife

305. Who says this?
"One cannot have too large a party. A large party secures its own amusement." (*Emma*)

A) Mr. Weston
B) Mrs. Elton
C) Miss Bates

306. In 2011, Ashley Williams starred as Elinor Dashwood in a movie adaptation of what name?

A) *Incense and Insensibility*
B) *Elinor and Edward*
C) *Scents and Sensibility*

307. *Northanger Abbey* makes an early reference to which sport?

A) baseball
B) golf
C) squash

308. Whom is being described?
"[He] had purchased independence by uniting himself to a rich woman of inferior birth."

A) Mr. Elliot (*Persuasion*)
B) Mr. Willoughby (*Sense and Sensibility*)
C) Mr. Elton (*Emma*)

309. Who said it?
"Miss Austen's novels are perfect works on a small scale—beautiful bits of stippling."

A) Matthew Arnold
B) Alfred, Lord Tennyson
C) Charles Dickens

310. Who saves Jane Fairfax's life? (*Emma*)

A) Frank Churchill
B) Mr. Dixon
C) Mr. Knightley

311. Who says this?
"I have no wish to be distinguished; and I have every reason to hope I never shall. Thank Heaven! I cannot be forced into genius and eloquence."

A) Mr. Wickham (*Pride and Prejudice*)
B) Captain Benwick (*Persuasion*)
C) Edward Ferrars (*Sense and Sensibility*)

312. What is the name of the Helen Fielding novel based loosely on *Pride and Prejudice*?

313. Which woman is NOT a sister to Lady Bertram? (*Mansfield Park*)

A) Mrs. Norris
B) Mrs. Price
C) Mrs. Grant

314. Whom does this describe?
"She was stronger alone; and her own good sense so well supported her, that her firmness was as unshaken."

A) Elinor Dashwood (*Sense and Sensibility*)
B) Fanny Price (*Mansfield Park*)
C) Anne Elliot (*Persuasion*)

315. Which Jane Austen novel was her personal favorite?

316. Where does Mrs. Smith live? (*Persuasion*)

A) Marlborough Buildings
B) Westgate Buildings
C) Camden Park

317. Who says this?
"[Mr. Bingley] may live in my memory as the most amiable man of my acquaintance, but that is all. I have nothing either to hope or fear, and nothing to reproach him with." (*Pride and Prejudice*)

318. In 1996, Joan Aiken attempted to complete *The Watsons* in a novel called _____.

A) *Emma Watson: The Watsons Completed*
B) *Husband Hunting*
C) *The Watsons and the Osbornes*

319. Which book was NOT mentioned in *Northanger Abbey*?

A) *Camilla*
B) *The Castle of Wolfenbach*
C) *Dracula*
D) *Tom Jones*

320. "[Anne Elliot] had given [Captain Wentworth] up to oblige others. It had been the effect of _____. It had been weakness and timidity."

A) manipulation
B) coercion
C) over-persuasion

321. Which famous woman popularized dresses with the Empire waist, which Jane Austen wore?

A) Joséphine de Beauharnais
B) Queen Charlotte
C) Frances Burney

322. Which of these couples marry first at the end of *Emma*?

A) Frank and Jane Churchill
B) Harriet and Robert Martin
C) Emma and George Knightley

323. Whom does this describe?
"The manner in which it was done so grossly uncivil, hurrying [Catherine] away without any reference to her own convenience, . . .as if resolved to have her gone before he was stirring in the morning, that he might not be obliged even to see her."

A) John Thorpe
B) Mr. Allen
C) General Tilney

324. True or false?

Both Emma Thompson and Kate Winslet were nominated for Academy Awards for their portrayals of Elinor and Marianne Dashwood, respectively.

325. What did Lady Bertram say she would give Fanny? (*Mansfield Park*)

A) a shawl from the East Indies
B) some pheasant eggs
C) a puppy from her pug's next litter

326. Which heroine was Jane Austen talking about?
"I think her as delightful a creature as ever appeared in print."

A) Elizabeth Bennet
B) Emma Woodhouse
C) Fanny Price

327. Which Scottish town was famous for being a place couples from England would elope to?

328. Why does Isabella Thorpe ultimately reject James Morland? (*Northanger Abbey*)

A) She realized he's not very rich.
B) He embarrassed her at a ball.
C) Her brother convinced her to call off the engagement.

329. Who says this?
"I wish. . .that somebody would give us a large fortune a-piece!"

A) Margaret Dashwood (*Sense and Sensibility*)
B) Elizabeth Elliot (*Persuasion*)
C) Lydia Bennet (*Pride and Prejudice*)

330. Alexander McCall Smith rewrote which Jane Austen novel with a modern twist?

A) *Pride and Prejudice*
B) *Emma*
C) *Persuasion*

331. What is the implied connection between Mr. Elliot and Mrs. Clay in *Persuasion*?

A) They are siblings.
B) They are blackmailing Sir Walter Elliot.
C) They are courting secretly.

332. Who says this?
"There is no drinking at Oxford now, I assure you. . . You would hardly meet with a man who goes beyond his four pints at the utmost."

A) John Thorpe (*Northanger Abbey*)
B) Tom Bertram (*Mansfield Park*)
C) John Willoughby (*Sense and Sensibility*)

333. Who said it?

"[Jane Austen] is in my opinion one of the half dozen greatest English writers."

A) Zadie Smith
B) Daniel Mendelsohn
C) Edmund Wilson

334. Who is expecting a baby by the end of *Pride and Prejudice*?

A) Lydia Wickham
B) Elizabeth Darcy
C) Charlotte Collins

335. Whom does this describe?
"She had not been brought up to understand the propensities of a rattle, nor to know to how many idle assertions and impudent falsehoods the excess of vanity will lead." (*Northanger Abbey*)

A) Isabella Thorpe
B) Catherine Morland
C) Eleanor Tilney

336. In 2011, Jonathan Dove created a version of *Mansfield Park* in the form of _____.

A) a video game
B) an opera
C) a radio play

337. Why did Colonel Brandon need to fetch Mrs. Dashwood in a hurry? (*Sense and Sensibility*)

A) Marianne was seriously ill.
B) He was ready to marry Marianne.
C) Margaret had an accident.

338. Which character was Jane Austen talking about when she said this?
"I am going to take a heroine whom no one but myself will much like."

A) Emma Woodhouse (*Emma*)
B) Fanny Price (*Mansfield Park*)
C) Lady Susan Vernon (*Lady Susan*)

339. True or false?

In Jane Austen's day, a bride and groom would only kiss on the cheek at their wedding.

340. Where does Mr. Elliot tell Anne he is going, only to be seen meeting Mrs. Clay instead? (*Persuasion*)

A) to Laura Place
B) out of Bath
C) to a local inn

341. Whom does this describe?
"She was reasonable enough to allow that a man of five and thirty might well have outlived all acuteness of feeling and every exquisite power of enjoyment."

A) Henrietta Musgrove (*Persuasion*)
B) Marianne Dashwood (*Sense and Sensibility*)
C) Emma Woodhouse (*Emma*)

342. An Assembly Such as This (Pamela Aidan, 2003) is a retelling of the beginning of *Pride and Prejudice* from whose perspective?

A) Mr. Bingley's
B) Jane Bennet's
C) Mr. Darcy's

343. In which book does the following quote appear?
"A woman especially, if she have the misfortune of knowing anything, should conceal it as well as she can."

A) *Northanger Abbey*
B) *Persuasion*
C) *Mansfield Park*

344. Who says this?
"I was quiet, but I was not blind. I could not but see that Mr. Crawford allowed himself in gallantries which did mean nothing."
(*Mansfield Park*)

A) Fanny Price
B) Edmund Bertram
C) Maria Bertram

345. Which one of Jane Austen's brothers fought in the Napoleonic Wars?

A) Henry
B) Frank
C) James

346. Where does Emma finally meet Frank Churchill?

A) at Hartfield
B) at Randalls
C) at Donwell Abbey

347. Whom does this describe?
"So far all was perfectly right; but [she] was almost startled by the wrong of one part of the Kellynch Hall plan, when it burst on her, which was, Mrs Clay's being engaged to go to Bath with Sir Walter and Elizabeth." (*Persuasion*)

A) Mary Musgrove
B) Sophia Croft
C) Lady Russell

348. Which novel was the book *Bridget Jones: The Edge of* Reason (Helen Fielding, 1999) loosely based on?

A) *Mansfield Park*
B) *Sense and Sensibility*
C) *Persuasion*

349. Jane Fairfax will become a _____ if she doesn't marry. (*Emma*)

A) governess
B) seamstress
C) maid

350. Whom is Lady Susan talking to?
"My dear _____, of what a mistake were you guilty in marrying a man of his age! Just old enough to be formal, ungovernable, and to have the gout; too old to be agreeable, too young to die."

A) Lady De Courcy
B) Alicia Johnson
C) Frederica Vernon

351. In Jane's day, who would often accompany newlyweds on their honeymoon?

A) a single female friend/relative of the bride
B) the bride's mother
C) a married relative of the bride

Set 15
Answers on pg. 187

---

352. How did Mrs. Tilney die? (*Northanger Abbey*)

A) at her husband's hand
B) a fever and seizure
C) a terrible accident

---

353. Who says this?
"I am sure [my husband] would like a place at court very much, and I do not think we shall have quite money enough to live upon without some help."

A) Charlotte Palmer (*Sense and Sensibility*)
B) Lydia Bennet Wickham (*Pride and Prejudice*)
C) Isabella Thorpe (*Northanger Abbey*)

---

354. Ben H. Winters combined *Sense and Sensibility* and which mythological creatures to create a parody novel?

A) minotaurs
B) cyclopes
C) sea monsters

---

355. Which instrument has Fanny Price never heard, but wishes to hear? (*Mansfield Park*)

A) a Broadwood grand piano
B) the harp
C) the cello

356. Who says this?

"Now I must give one smirk, and then we may be rational again."

A) Mr. Bingley (*Pride and Prejudice*)
B) Mr. Willoughby (*Sense and Sensibility*)
C) Henry Tilney (*Northanger Abbey*)

357. Who said it?

". . .you've got to be a Janeite in your 'heart. You take it from me, there's no one to touch Jane when you're in a tight place."

A) Margaret Mitchell
B) Robert Louis Stevenson
C) Rudyard Kipling

358. What is the housekeeper's name that Henry mentions in his Gothic horror story? (*Northanger Abbey*)

A) Molly
B) Dorothy
C) Anna

359. Who says this?
"Upon my honour I never met with so many pleasant girls in my life, as I have this evening; and there are several of them, you see, uncommonly pretty."

A) Robert Ferrars (*Sense and Sensibility*)
B) Mr. Elton (*Emma*)
C) Mr. Bingley (*Pride and Prejudice*)

360. Which character does Daniel Vincent Gordh play in *The Lizzie Bennet Diaries*?

A) William Darcy
B) Bing Lee
C) Ricky Collins

361. Whom is Robert Ferrars related to? (*Sense and Sensibility*)

A) Fanny Dashwood
B) Charlotte Palmer
C) Mr. Willoughby

362. Whom does this describe?
"His two other children [besides Elizabeth] were of very inferior value."

A) Mr. Watson (*The Watsons*)
B) Sir Walter Elliot (*Persuasion*)
C) Mr. Bennet (*Pride and Prejudice*)

363. Immediately after Jane's father's death, where in Bath did she and her sister move to?

A) Gay Street
B) College Street
C) Henrietta Street

364. Which character smells of alcohol? (*Pride and Prejudice*)

A) Captain Denny
B) Mr. Phillips
C) Mr. Hurst

365. Whom does this describe?
"[He] had not much to recommend him beyond habits of fashion and expense, and being the younger son of a lord with a tolerable independence; and Sir Thomas would probably have thought his introduction at Mansfield by no means desirable." (*Mansfield Park*)

A) John Yates
B) Mr. Rushworth
C) Henry Crawford

366. Who wrote the screenplay for the mini-series of *Emma* (2009)?

A) Andrew Davies
B) Sandy Welch
C) Heidi Thomas

---

367. What is the name of the Ann Radcliffe novel Catherine reads? (*Northanger Abbey*)

A) *The Castle of Otranto*
B) *The Monk*
C) *The Mysteries of Udolpho*

---

368. Whom does this describe?
". . .marriage had always been her object; it was the only honourable provision for well-educated young women of small fortune, . . .however uncertain of giving happiness. . ."

A) Charlotte Lucas (*Pride and Prejudice*)
B) Harriet Smith (*Emma*)
C) Isabella Thorpe (*Northanger Abbey*)

---

369. In Jane's day, how many women would die in childbirth per day in England?

A) seven
B) nine
C) eleven

---

370. "[Mrs. Ferrars'] dinner was a grand one ...—no poverty of any kind, except of _____, appeared—but there, the deficiency was considerable." (*Sense and Sensibility*)

A) entertainment
B) manners
C) conversation

371. Who says this to Emma?
"It was badly done, indeed! . . . I must, I will,–I will tell you truths while I can." (*Emma*)

A) Mr. Woodhouse
B) Mr. Knightley
C) Mr. Elton

372. In the movie *The Jane Austen Book Club* (2007), the characters go to the cinema to watch which movie adaptation?

A) *Persuasion*
B) *Pride and Prejudice*
C) *Mansfield Park*

373. What is Mr. Shepherd's profession? (*Persuasion*)

A) banker
B) real estate agent
C) lawyer

374. Whom does this describe?
"[She] resigned herself to the idea of it, with all the philosophy of a well bred woman, contenting herself with merely giving her husband a gentle reprimand on the subject five or six times every day."

A) Lady Middleton (*Sense and Sensibility*)
B) Mrs. Bennet (*Pride and Prejudice*)
C) Augusta Elton (*Emma*)

375. In total, how much did Jane Austen make from her novels in her lifetime?

A) £700
B) £7000
C) £70,000

376. Why does Wickham want to leave Brighton in a hurry?
(*Pride and Prejudice*)

A) He wants to escape military life.
B) He has too many gambling debts.
C) He is anxious to marry Lydia.

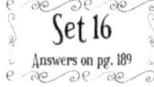

---

377. Whom does this describe?
"The shawl which Edmund was quietly taking from the servant to bring and put round her shoulders was seized by [Henry]'s quicker hand, and she was obliged to be indebted to his more prominent attention."
(*Mansfield Park*)

A) Maria Bertram
B) Fanny Price
C) Mary Crawford

---

378. Joanna David, who played Mrs. Gardiner in the 1995 version of *Pride and Prejudice*, is the real-life mother of the actress who played _____ in the same series.

A) Lydia Bennet
B) Georgiana Darcy
C) Anne de Bourgh

---

379. Why does Frank Churchill show overt interest in Emma Woodhouse?
(*Emma*)

A) he needs to marry for money
B) to make Mr. Knightley jealous
C) to hide his true feelings for another

---

380. Who says this?
"I have been meditating on the very great pleasure which a pair of fine eyes in the face of a pretty woman can bestow."

A) Mr. Willoughby (*Sense and Sensibility*)
B) Mr. Darcy (*Pride and Prejudice*)
C) Frederick Tilney (*Northanger Abbey*)

---

381. Which writer admits she has read *Emma* "at least 20 times"?

A) J. K. Rowling
B) Helen Fielding
C) Margaret Atwood

382. Whom does John Dashwood encourage Elinor to "try for"?
(*Sense and Sensibility*)

A) Edward Ferrars
B) Colonel Brandon
C) John Willoughby

383. Who says this?
"I have no notion of treating men with such respect. That is the way to spoil them."

A) Isabella Thorpe (*Northanger Abbey*)
B) Mrs. Elton (*Emma*)
C) Caroline Bingley (*Pride and Prejudice*)

384. *Jane Austen in Scarsdale* (Paula Marantz Cohen) is a rewrite of which novel?

A) *Northanger Abbey*
B) *Emma*
C) *Persuasion*

385. What does Tom Bertram want Fanny to do for the play at Mansfield Park?

A) to make the curtain
B) to help Mr. Rushworth learn his lines
C) to play "Cottager's Wife"

386. Which heroine does this describe?

"She mediated, by turns, on broken promises and broken arches, phaetons and false hangings, Tilneys and trap-doors."

387. What did ladies and gentlemen wear at all times at a ball in Jane's day?

A) hats
B) scarves
C) gloves

388. Who "disappointed" Elizabeth Elliot in her youth? (*Persuasion*)

A) Charles Musgrove
B) Mr. William Elliot
C) Captain Wentworth

389. Whom is Emma talking about?
"It is very unfair to judge of any body's conduct, without an intimate knowledge of their situation. Nobody, who has not been in the interior of a family, can say what the difficulties of any individual of that family may be." (*Emma*)

A) Jane Fairfax
B) Harriet Smith
C) Frank Churchill

390. *Kandukondain Kandukondain* (2010) is an Indian movie version of which novel?

A) *Persuasion*
B) *Sense and Sensibility*
C) *Pride and Prejudice*

391. Why is Mrs. Gardiner familiar with Pemberley? (*Pride and Prejudice*)

A) She grew up near the estate.
B) She worked there when she was young.
C) Her father often talked of it.

392. Who says this?
"What is right to be done cannot be done too soon."

A) Admiral Croft (*Persuasion*)
B) Mr. Weston (*Emma*)
C) James Morland (*Northanger Abbey*)

393. Which novel was Jane Austen goaded into dedicating to the Prince of Wales—a man she detested?

394. Who is Miss Frances Ward?

A) Mr. Darcy's cousin (*Pride and Prejudice*)
B) Fanny Price's mother (*Mansfield Park*)
C) Catherine Morland's friend (*Northanger Abbey*)

395. Whom does this describe?
"[She observed] that Miss Morton was the daughter of a nobleman with thirty thousand pounds, while Miss Dashwood was only the daughter of a private gentleman with no more than three." (*Sense and Sensibility*)

A) Lucy Steele
B) Fanny Dashwood
C) Mrs. Ferrars

396. What is the title of a *Persuasion* rewrite that tells the same story from Captain Wentworth's perspective?

A) *A Heart Grows Fonder*
B) *Persuaded Once More*
C) *Captain Wentworth's Diary*

397. Which unfinished work was originally titled *The Brothers*?

A) *The Watsons*
B) *Sanditon*
C) *Lady Susan*

398. Who says this?
"In every congregation there is a larger proportion who know a little of the matter, and who can judge and criticise."

A) Edward Ferrars (*Sense and Sensibility*)
B) Edmund Bertram (*Mansfield Park*)
C) Mr. Collins (*Pride and Prejudice*)

399. True or false?

Jane Austen's brother Henry drew the only portrait we have of Jane.

400. Which author does Catherine read as a child? (*Northanger Abbey*)

A) Friedrich Schiller
B) Maria Edgworth
C) Thomas Gray

401. Whom does this describe?
"With the prospect of spending at least two months at Uppercross, it was highly incumbent on her to clothe her imagination, her memory, and all her ideas in as much of Uppercross as possible." (*Persuasion*)

A) Elizabeth Elliot
B) Mary Musgove
C) Anne Elliot

Set 17
Answers on pg. 191

402. Whose screenplay describes Mr. Darcy as looking "as if somebody has had a bad attack of wind"? (*Pride and Prejudice*)

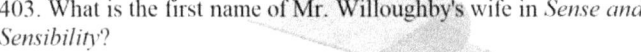

403. What is the first name of Mr. Willoughby's wife in *Sense and Sensibility*?

A) Augusta
B) Sophia
C) Georgiana

404. Who says this?
"No one can think more highly of the understanding of women than I do. In my opinion, nature has given them so much, that they never find it necessary to use more than half."

A) Henry Tilney (*Northanger Abbey*)
B) Mr. Bingley (*Pride and Prejudice*)
C) Captain Harville (*Persuasion*)

405. Who said it?
"But some characters in books are really real--Jane Austen's are."

A) Dodie Smith
B) Doris Lessing
C) Jean Rhys

406. How does Mr. Bennet initially feel about Elizabeth and Darcy's engagement? (*Pride and Prejudice*)

A) angry
B) skeptical
C) elated

---

407. Whom does this describe?
"Had he married a more amiable woman, he might even have been made amiable himself; for he was very young when he married, and very fond of his wife."

A) John Dashwood (*Sense and Sensibility*)
B) Mr. Elliot (*Persuasion*)
C) John Knightley (*Emma*)

---

408. What is the name of a 2010 Indian movie adaptation of *Emma*?

A) *Abha*
B) *Aisha*
C) *Amita*

---

409. Which of the following pairs of sisters aren't close?

A) Jane and Elizabeth Bennet (*Pride and Prejudice*)
B) Elinor and Marianne Dashwood (*Sense and Sensibility*)
C) Anne and Elizabeth Elliot (*Persuasion*)

---

410. Who says this?
"Those who do not complain are never pitied."

A) Mr. Palmer (*Sense and Sensibility*)
B) Mary Musgrove (*Persuasion*)
C) Mrs. Bennet (*Pride and Prejudice*)

411. How old was Jane when she wrote *Love and Freindship*?

A) 14
B) 15
C) 16

412. What does Mrs. Jennings think when Colonel Brandon tells Elinor he has a living to offer Edward? (*Sense and Sensibility*)

A) That they are discussing his ward Eliza.
B) That he's making an offer of marriage to Elinor.
C) That he's professing his intentions to court Marianne.

413. Which man is Mr. Knightley talking about?
"There is one thing, Emma, which a man can always do, if he chuses, and that is, his duty; not by maneuvering and finessing, but by vigour and resolution." (*Emma*)

A) Mr. Elton
B) Mr. Weston
C) Frank Churchill

414. Who is the author of the murder mystery *Death Comes to Pemberley*?

A) Anne Perry
B) P.D. James
C) Patricia Highsmith

415. What type of play did Tom Bertram prefer to be performed at Mansfield Park?

A) tragic
B) comic
C) Shakespearean

416. Who wrote this in a letter?
"Dare not say that man forgets sooner than woman, that his love has an earlier death. I have loved none but you."

A) Captain Wentworth (*Persuasion*)
B) Mr. Darcy (*Pride and Prejudice*)
C) Mr. Knightley (*Emma*)

417. What year did Jane Austen die?

A) 1817
B) 1819
C) 1821

418. What does Catherine find in Mrs. Tilney's room that captures her interest? (*Northanger Abbey*)

A) an old letter
B) a map
C) nothing

419. Who says this?
"I am not romantic, you know; I never was. I ask only a comfortable home."

A) Jane Fairfax (*Emma*)
B) Charlotte Lucas (*Pride and Prejudice*)
C) Henrietta Musgrove (*Persuasion*)

420. Who played Mr. Willoughby in the 2008 BBC version of *Sense and Sensibility*?

A) Dominic Cooper
B) David Morrissey
C) Dan Stevens

421. Which work was NOT included in Jane's *Juvenilia*?

A) *Lady Susan*
B) *The History of England*
C) *Love and Freindship*

422. Whom does this describe?
"[She], handsome, clever, and rich, with a comfortable home and happy disposition, . . .had lived nearly twenty-one years in the world with very little to distress or vex her."

A) Mary Crawford (*Mansfield Park*)
B) Elizabeth Bennet (*Pride and Prejudice*)
C) Emma Woodhouse (*Emma*)

423. Which American pop star purchased Jane Austen's ring, then was told it was too "historical" to leave England?

A) Kelly Clarkson
B) Miley Cyrus
C) Paris Hilton

424. Who is Mrs. Clay's father? (*Persuasion*)

A) Admiral Croft
B) Mr. Shepherd
C) Mr. Musgrove

425. Whom is Edward Ferrars talking about?
"I know her greatness of soul, there would not be music enough in London to content her." (*Sense and Sensibility*)

A) Fanny Dashwood
B) Elinor Dashwood
C) Marianne Dashwood

426. Which novel refers to a passage from *Northanger Abbey* in its preface?

A) *Atonement* (Ian McEwan)
B) *Possession* (A.S. Byatt)
C) *The Blind Assassin* (Margaret Atwood)

Set 18
Answers on pg. 193

427. Who is Mr. Wickham to Mr. Darcy? (*Pride and Prejudice*)

A) his former business partner
B) the son of his father's employee
C) a second cousin

428. Who says this?
"Be honest and poor, by all means-but I shall not envy you; I do not much think I shall even respect you. I have a much greater respect for those that are honest and rich."

A) Mary Crawford (*Mansfield Park*)
B) Lucy Steele (*Sense and Sensibility*)
C) Caroline Bingley (*Pride and Prejudice*)

429. Who said it?
"Every time I read *Pride and Prejudice,* I want to dig [Jane Austen] up and hit her over the head with her own shin bone."

A) Ernest Hemingway
B) Mark Twain
C) Joseph Conrad

430. What sum of money was left to the Dashwood girls by their great uncle upon his death? (*Sense and Sensibility*)

A) £500 apiece
B) £1000 apiece
C) nothing

431. Whom is John Thorpe talking to?
"Where did you get that quiz of a hat? It makes you look like an old witch."
(*Northanger Abbey*)

A) Mrs. Thorpe
B) Mrs. Morland
C) Mrs. Allen

432. Which "sequel" to *Persuasion* involves time-travelling in Bath?

A) *Captain Wentworth's Persuasion*
B) *Searching for Captain Wentworth*
C) *Mercy's Embrace: The Elizabeth Elliot Story*

433. Who was Mr. Weston's first wife? (*Emma*)

A) Miss Goddard
B) Miss Dixon
C) Miss Churchill

434. Who says this?
"People who suffer as I do from nervous complaints can have no great
inclination for talking. Nobody can tell what I suffer!"

A) Mr. Woodhouse (*Emma*)
B) Mrs. Bennet (*Pride and Prejudice*)
C) Lady Bertram (*Mansfield Park*)

435. Which original Jane Austen manuscript was sold at Sotheby's
for £850,000 in 2011?

A) *The Watsons*
B) *Lady Susan*
C) *Sanditon*

436. Which character is the wealthiest? (*Northanger Abbey*)

A) Mrs. Thorpe
B) Mr. Allen
C) General Tilney

437. Whom is Mary Musgrove talking about?
"I cannot think him at all a fit match for Henrietta; and considering the alliances which the Musgroves have made, she has no right to throw herself away." (*Persuasion*)

A) Captain Wentworth
B) Captain Benwick
C) Charles Hayter

438. What is the name of a comic strip involving Jane Austen characters saying things supporting men's rights?

A) *Manfeels Park*
B) *Sex and Sensibility*
C) *Pride and Pectorals*

439. Where did Fanny Price go for refuge after Henry Crawford's proposal? (*Mansfield Park*)

A) the East Room
B) the White Attic
C) the garden

440. Whom does this describe?

"Her mind did become settled, but it was settled in a gloomy dejection. She felt the loss of Willoughby's character yet more heavily than she had felt the loss of his heart. . ."

441. Before tea and toast became the typical breakfast of ladies and gentlemen, what did a traditional breakfast consist of?

A) bread and cheese
B) oats and honey
C) cold beef and alcohol

442. How does the group at Lyme figure out who Mr. Elliot is? (*Persuasion*)

A) The locals inform them.
B) He introduces himself on the beach.
C) Anne immediately recognizes him.

443. Whom does this describe?
"She had a husband whose warm heart and sweet temper made him think every thing due to her in return for the great goodness of being in love with him."(*Emma*)

A) Mr. Weston's first wife
B) Isabella Knightley
C) Mrs. Woodhouse

444. *The Independence of Miss Mary Bennet* is a "sequel" written by which author?

A) Margaret Murray
B) Siobhan Dowd
C) Colleen McCullough

445. Who is Lady Susan's close confidant? (*Lady Susan*)

A) Maria Manwaring
B) Miss Summers
C) Alicia Johnson

446. Who says this?
"Let me entreat you never to think of him again, my dear Catherine;
indeed he is unworthy of you." (*Northanger Abbey*)

A) Isabella Thorpe
B) Mrs. Allen
C) Eleanor Tilney

447. In Jane's day, why would an unmarried girl take a slice of
cake home from a wedding?

A) She would put it under her pillow.
B) She would give it to the boy she liked.
C) She would save it for a year.

448. What does Mrs. Norris not have the least intention of
doing? (*Mansfield Park*)

A) Acquire a cream cheese from Southerton.
B) Have Fanny Price live with her.
C) Fit up a curtain out of green baise.

449. Whom does this describe?
"He had left the girl whose youth and innocence he had seduced, in a
situation of the utmost distress, with no creditable home, no help, no
friends, ignorant of his address!"

A) John Thorpe (*Northanger Abbey*)
B) Henry Crawford (*Mansfield Park*)
C) Mr. Willoughby (*Sense and Sensibility*)

450. *Persuasion* is referenced in which novel by John Fowles?

A) *Shipwreck*
B) *The French Lieutenant's Woman*
C) *The Ebony Tower*

451. Frank Churchill rescues Harriet Smith from _____.
(*Emma*)

A) a run-away horse
B) the embarrassment of not dancing at a ball
C) gypsies

452. Who says this?
"An engaged woman is always more agreeable than a disengaged. . .
All is safe with a lady engaged: no harm can be done."

A) Frank Churchill (*Emma*)
B) Frederick Tilney (*Northanger Abbey*)
C) Henry Crawford (*Mansfield Park*)

453. "The celestial brightness of _____ is unequalled even
in Jane Austen's other work." (Elizabeth Jenkins)

A) *Sense and Sensibility*
B) *Pride and Prejudice*
C) *Persuasion*

454. After the dinner with Mrs. Ferrars, what "one subject only
engaged the ladies till coffee came in"?

A) balls and parties in London
B) politics in their variety
C) the comparative heights of Harry Dashwood and William
Middleton

455. Whom does this describe?
"[She] had been an excellent woman, sensible and amiable; . . .--She
had humoured, or softened, or concealed [Sir Walter's] failings, and
promoted his real respectability for seventeen years." (*Persuasion*)

A) Lady Dalrymple
B) Lady Elliot
C) Lady Russell

456. Where does the action of Ibi Zaboi's book adaptation (*Pride*, 2018) of *Pride and Prejudice* take place?

A) Zimbabwe
B) Brooklyn, New York
C) Chicago, Illinois

457. What was *Northanger Abbey* originally called?

A) *Susan*
B) *Catherine*
C) *Isabella*

458. Who says this?
"People always live forever when there is an annuity to be paid them . . ."

A) Fanny Dashwood (*Sense and Sensibility*)
B) Sir Thomas Bertram (*Mansfield Park*)
C) Mr. Darcy (*Pride and Prejudice*)

459. Which character in *Pride and Prejudice* had a "personality makeover" to fit French sensibilities before publication in France in 1813?

460. Whom does this describe?
"Except her being so dull, [Lady Bertram] must add she saw no harm in the poor little thing- and always found her very handy and quick in carrying messages, and fetching what she wanted."

A) Harriet Smith (*Emma*)
B) Lucy Steele (*Sense and Sensibility*)
C) Fanny Price (*Mansfield Park*)

461. Whom does this describe?
"Always to be presented with the date of her own birth and see no marriage follow but that of a youngest sister, made the [family] book an evil." (*Persuasion*)

A) Elizabeth Elliot
B) Anne Elliot
C) Louisa Musgrove

462. Which American actress played Emma in the 1996 theatrical movie of the same name?

463. How does Captain Wentworth sign his letter at the end of *Persuasion*?

A) F.W.
B) F. Wentworth
C) Frederick

464. Who says it?
". . .we must stem the tide of malice, and pour into the wounded bosoms of each other, the balm of sisterly consolation."

A) Marianne Dashwood (*Sense and Sensibility*)
B) Julia Bertram (*Mansfield Park*)
C) Mary Bennet (*Pride and Prejudice*)

465. In Jane Austen's day, the banns were required to be "published" how many Sundays before a wedding (that is, unless a special license were acquired)?

A) 3
B) 6
C) 8

466. Where does James propose to Isabella? (*Northanger Abbey*)

A) on a walk by Beechen Cliff
B) at the Allens' dinner party
C) in a carriage

467. Who says this?
"I hope you will like the chain itself, Fanny. . . I know you will be kind to my intentions, and consider it, as it really is, a token of the love of one of your oldest friends." (*Mansfield Park*)

A) John Yates
B) Edmund Bertram
C) Henry Crawford

468. Which unfinished Austen novel was controversially adapted into a series by Andrew Davies in 2019?

A) *The Watsons*
B) *Sanditon*
C) *Lady Susan*

469. What is the name of Mrs. Smith's late husband? (*Persuasion*)

A) John
B) William
C) Charles

470. Whom does this describe?
"He seemed to be about four or five and twenty, was rather tall, had a pleasing countenance, a very intelligent and lively eye, and, if not quite handsome, was very near it."

A) Captain Wentworth (*Persuasion*)
B) Mr. Darcy (*Pride and Prejudice*)
C) Henry Tilney (*Northanger Abbey*)

471. What tragic event occurred on Jane Austen's 29th birthday?

A) the death of a friend
B) a declaration of war
C) her family announcing they would move

472. In reference to "the matrimonial state," what word does Henry Crawford dwell on when he considers the blessings of a wife as "Heaven's last best gift"? (*Mansfield Park*)

A) best
B) last
C) Heaven's
D) gift

473. Whom does this describe?
"[She], weak-spirited, irritable, and completely under Lydia's guidance, had been always affronted by [her parents'] advice." (*Pride and Prejudice*)

A) Jane Bennet
B) Mary Bennet
C) Kitty Bennet

474. Who wrote the updated version of *Sense and Sensibility* for The Austen Project?

A) Penelope Ward
B) Joanna Trollope
C) Colleen Hoover

475. Where does the ball in *Emma* take place?

A) Donwell Abbey
B) the Crown Inn
C) Hartfield

476. Who says this to Anne Elliot? (*Persuasion*)
"[Mr. Elliot] truly wants to marry you. His present attentions to your family are very sincere: quite from the heart."

A) Lady Russell
B) Mrs. Clay
C) Mrs. Smith

477. Who said it?
"[Jane Austen is] the most perfect artist among women."

A) Virginia Woolf
B) Ellen Glasgow
C) Gertrude Stein

478. What was the Tilney residence formerly used as? (*Northanger Abbey*)

A) a convent
B) a school
C) a hotel

479. Whom does this describe?
"[She] could sit still no longer. She almost ran out of the room, and as soon as the door was closed, burst into tears of joy, which at first she thought would never cease." (*Sense and Sensibility*)

A) Elinor Dashwood
B) Marianne Dashwood
C) Margaret Dashwood

480. Which Austen novel was NOT adapted into a comic book for Marvel Comics?

A) *Pride and Prejudice*
B) *Persuasion*
C) *Sense and Sensibility*
D) *Emma*

481. What kind of exercise does Fanny Price enjoy most?
(*Mansfield Park*)

A) long walks
B) hiking
C) riding

482. Who says this?
"Young ladies are delicate plants. They should take care of their
health and their complexion."

A) Mrs. Allen (*Northanger Abbey*)
B) Mr. Bennet (*Pride and Prejudice*)
C) Mr. Woodhouse (*Emma*)

483. True or false?

At a dinner party in Jane's time, guests would often criticize the
performance of the servants during dinner.

484. Where does Charles Hayter live? (*Persuasion*)

A) Uppercross
B) Lyme
C) Winthrop

485. Who says this?
"Where pride and stupidity unite there can be no dissimulation
worthy notice."

A) Reginald De Courcy (*Lady Susan*)
B) Sir Edward Denham (*Sanditon*)
C) Tom Musgrave (*The Watsons*)

486. In 2013, Chicago's Remy Bumppo Theatre featured a stage adaptation of which novel?

A) *Persuasion*
B) *Sense and Sensibility*
C) *Northanger Abbey*

487. Who can call Combe Magna home? (*Sense and Sensibility*)

A) Colonel Brandon
B) Mr. Willoughby
C) Sir John Middleton

488. Whom does this describe?
"She was a woman of mean understanding, little information, and uncertain temper."

A) Mrs. Jennings (*Sense and Sensibility*)
B) Mrs. Bennet (*Pride and Prejudice*)
C) Lady Dalrymple (*Persuasion*)

489. True or false?

Jane Austen's family often put on theatricals such as the one featured in *Mansfield Park*.

490. What is the name of Mr. Weston's estate? (*Emma*)

A) Maple Grove
B) Donwell Abbey
C) Randalls

491. Whom does this describe?
"I have very little to say for [his] motives,. . . He has his vanities as well as Miss Thorpe, and the chief difference is, that, having a stronger head, they have not yet injured himself." (*Northanger Abbey*)

A) James Morland
B) Henry Tilney
C) Frederick Tilney

492. In *Revisit Mansfield Park* (Sarah Ozcandarli, 2014), what is the major plot difference between the original and the rewrite?

A) Edmund Bertram marries Mary Crawford
B) Fanny Price marries Henry Crawford
C) Julia Bertram marries Mr. Rushworth

493. What are the closing words to *Persuasion*?

A) "But, in spite of these deficiencies, the wishes, the hopes, the confidence, the predictions of the small band of true friends. . ."
B) "And they were both ever sensible of the warmest gratitude towards the persons, who, by bringing her into Derbyshire. . ."
C) "She gloried in being a sailor's wife. . ."

494. Who says this?
"I did not know I contradicted anybody in calling your mother ill-bred."

A) Mr. Darcy (*Pride and Prejudice*)
B) Mary Crawford (*Mansfield Park*)
C) Mr. Palmer (*Sense and Sensibility*)

495. True or false?

In Jane Austen's day, church attendance was higher in the cities than in the country.

496. Who says this?
"I shall be most happy to play to you both, at least as long as you can like to listen: probably much longer, for I dearly love music myself."

A) Mary Crawford (*Mansfield Park*)
B) Georgiana Darcy (*Pride and Prejudice*)
C) Marianne Dashwood (*Sense and Sensibility*)

497. Whom is Mr. Knightley talking about?
"I love to look at her; and I will add this praise, that I do not think her personally vain. Considering how handsome she is, she appears to be little occupied with it; her vanity lies another way." (*Emma*)

A) Jane Fairfax
B) Emma Woodhouse
C) Harriet Smith

498. *For Darkness Shows the Stars* (Diana Peterfreund, 2012) is a post-apocalyptic version of which Austen novel?

A) *Mansfield Park*
B) *Northanger Abbey*
C) *Persuasion*

499. When Isabella Thorpe makes a list of books for Catherine Morland to read, what did Catherine ask to make sure she would like them? (*Northanger Abbey*)

A) "Are they all romantic?"
B) "Are they all historical?"
C) "Are they all horrid?"

500. Whom does this describe?
"He was not handsome, and his manners required intimacy to make them pleasing. . .when his natural shyness was overcome, his behaviour gave every indication of an open, affectionate heart."

A) Edward Ferrars (*Sense and Sensibility*)
B) Robert Martin (*Emma*)
C) Edmund Bertram (*Mansfield Park*)

501. Who said it?
"I am at a loss to understand why people hold Miss Austen's novels at so high a rate."

A) Thomas Hardy
B) Lewis Carroll
C) Ralph Waldo Emerson

502. Whom does Harriet Smith NOT develop feelings for? (*Emma*)

A) Mr. Elton
B) Mr. Martin
C) Mr. Knightley
D) Frank Churchill

503. Whom is Lydia Bennet talking about?
"He never cared three straws about [Mary King] -- who could about such a nasty little freckled thing?" (*Pride and Prejudice*)

A) Mr. Collins
B) Mr. Bingley
C) Mr. Wickham

504. *From Mansfield with Love* is an adaptation of *Mansfield Park* in the form of _____.

A) a song
B) a vlog
C) a stage play

505. Why does Mrs. Musgrove feel a special connection to Captain Wentworth? (*Persuasion*)

A) He has traveled to the East Indies.
B) He was captain over her late son.
C) He attended school with her husband.

506. Whom does this describe?
"[She is] one of those well-meaning people who are always doing mistaken and very disagreeable things."

A) Mrs. Jennings (*Sense and Sensibility*)
B) Lady Russell (*Persuasion*)
C) Mrs. Norris (*Mansfield Park*)

507. Which instrument did Jane Austen play?

508. Which of the Watson daughters is a "spinster"? (*The Watsons*)

A) Penelope
B) Margaret
C) Elizabeth
D) Emma

509. Whom does this describe?
"Darkness impenetrable and immovable filled the room. A violent gust of wind, rising with sudden fury, added fresh horror to the moment. [She] trembled from head to foot."

A) Catherine Morland (*Northanger Abbey*)
B) Mary Musgrove (*Persuasion*)
C) Marianne Dashwood (*Sense and Sensibility*)

510. The novel *Longbourn* (Jo Baker, 2014) tells the story of the servants in the household of which novel?

511. What is the name of Mr. Willoughby's aunt's estate? (*Sense and Sensibility*)

A) Norland Park
B) Delaford
C) Allenham

512. Who said it?
"It appears to me that the usual style of letter-writing among women is faultless, except in three particulars. . .: a general deficiency of subject, a total inattention to stops, and a very frequent ignorance of grammar."

A) Mr. Darcy (*Pride and Prejudice*)
B) Mr. Knightley (*Emma*)
C) Henry Tilney (*Northanger Abbey*)

513. Which denomination of note does Jane Austen now appear on?

A) £10
B) £20
C) £50

514. Which of the following worries Mr. Woodhouse? (*Emma*)

A) having enough money
B) chicken thieves
C) finding a new wife

515. Which "couple" does this describe?
"He had nothing to do, and she had hardly anybody to love; but the encounter of such lavish recommendations could not fail. They were gradually acquainted, and when acquainted, rapidly and deeply in love."

A) Anne Elliot and Captain Wentworth
B) Catherine Morland and Henry Tilney
C) Marianne Dashwood and Mr. Willoughby

516. Which *Downton Abbey* actress appears in the film *Pride and Prejudice and Zombies* (2016)?

A) Lily James
B) Joanna Froggatt
C) Michelle Dockery

517. Which of the following characters is an adulteress?

A) Lydia Bennet (*Pride and Prejudice*)
B) Maria Bertram (*Mansfield Park*)
C) Charlotte Palmer (*Sense and Sensibility*)

518. Who says this?
"A single woman, of good fortune, is always respectable, and may be as sensible and pleasant as anybody else."

A) Emma Woodhouse (*Emma*)
B) Elizabeth Elliot (*Persuasion*)
C) Caroline Bingley (*Pride and Prejudice*)

519. Which famous collection of sermons, popular in Jane Austen's day, taught young women how to behave?

520. Why did the family of Sir Walter Elliot feel snubbed by Mr. Elliot in the past? (*Persuasion*)

A) He failed to visit after Mrs. Elliots' death.
B) He didn't invite them to his dinner party.
C) He didn't repay money they lent him.

521. Who says this?
"I was snowed up at a friend's house once for a week. Nothing could be pleasanter. I went for only one night, and could not get away till that very day se'nnight." (*Emma*)

A) Mr. Elton
B) Frank Churchill
C) Harriet Smith

522. In 2016, UDON Entertainment published *Sense and Sensibility* in the form of _____.

A) a web series
B) manga
C) a video game

523. What is the name of the village where the Morlands live and where Mr. Allen "owned the chief of the property"? (*Northanger Abbey*)

A) Meryton
B) Fullerton
C) Sotherton

524. Whom does this describe?
". . . it was not in her nature to question the veracity of a young man of such amiable appearance as Wickham." (*Pride and Prejudice*)

A) Jane Bennet
B) Mrs. Bennet
C) Lydia Bennet

525. Who said it?
"Stupid people sometimes complain that there is no sex in Austen's novels. . . Actual sexual intercourse is the off-stage climax of the Austen novel."

A) Germaine Greer
B) Gloria Steinham
C) Sue Townsend

526. What is the name of a play written by Jane in her youth?

A) "The Adventures of Mr. Harley"
B) "The Visit"
C) "Catherine, or the Bower"

527. Whom does this describe?
"His regard for her, infinitely surpassing anything that Willoughby ever felt or feigned. . .has subsisted through all the knowledge of dear Marianne's unhappy prepossession for that worthless young man!" (*Sense and Sensibility*)

A) Thomas Palmer
B) Edward Ferrars
C) Colonel Brandon

528. What is the name of the book by Emma Campbell Webster that allowed readers to choose where the story goes in the Austen realm?

A) *Lost in Austen*
B) *Pride and. . .Sensibility?*
C) *An Austen Adventure*

529. What does Mr. Elliot ask Anne to translate? (*Persuasion*)

A) a French hymn
B) an Italian aria
C) a Latin transcription

530. Who says this?
"If I loved you less, I might be able to talk about it more. But you know what I am. —You hear nothing but truth from me."

A) Henry Tilney (*Northanger Abbey*)
B) Edward Ferrars (*Sense and Sensibility*)
C) Mr. Knightley (*Emma*)

531. Henry Austen said, "Jane was fond of _____, and excelled in it."

A) dancing
B) card playing
C) croquet

532. Who locates Lydia and Wickham in London? (*Pride and Prejudice*)

A) Mr. Gardiner
B) Mr. Bennet
C) Mr. Darcy

533. Whom does this describe?
"Her uncle's anger gave her the severest pain of all. Selfish and ungrateful! To have appeared so to him! She was miserable for ever."

A) Fanny Price (*Mansfield Park*)
B) Elizabeth Bennet (*Pride and Prejudice*)
C) Anne Elliot (*Persuasion*)

534. Which novel quotes the final sentence from *Northanger Abbey* in its epigraph?

A) *The Last Unicorn* (Peter S. Beagle)
B) *Watership Down* (Richard Adams)
C) *Flowers for Algernon* (Daniel Keyes)

535. What item does Edward possess that puzzles the Dashwood sisters? (*Sense and Sensibility*)

A) a ring made of hair
B) a mini-portrait
C) an embroidered handkerchief

536. Whom does this describe?
"She was a manager by necessity, without any. . .inclination for it, or any. . .activity. Her disposition was indolent."

A) Mrs. Price (*Mansfield Park*)
B) Mrs. Bennet (*Pride and Prejudice*)
C) Mrs. Dashwood (*Sense and Sensibility*)

537. True or false?

In Jane's day, wedding bands were worn by both the bride and the groom.

538. Why does Charlotte agree to marry Mr. Collins? (*Pride and Prejudice*)

A) For his love and affection.
B) For the comfortable home he can offer.
C) For his connections to Lady Catherine.

539. Which heroine is this passage referring to?
"It must be very improper that a young lady should dream of a gentleman before the gentleman is first known to have dreamt of her."

A) Marianne Dashwood (*Sense and Sensibility*)
B) Catherine Morland (*Northanger Abbey*)
C) Emma Woodhouse (*Emma*)

540. Whit Stillman's 2016 film *Love and Friendship* is an adaption of which Austen work?

A) *Lady Susan*
B) *Love and Freindship*
C) *The Watsons*

541. What is the second Mrs. Weston's maiden name? (*Emma*)

A) Taylor
B) Smith
C) Churchill

542. Who says this?
"One cannot be always laughing at a man without now and then stumbling on something witty."

A) Susan Vernon (*Lady Susan*)
B) Elizabeth Bennet (*Pride and Prejudice*)
C) Lucy Steele (*Sense and Sensibility*)

543. Which date is Jane Austen's birthday?

A) December 16, 1775
B) July 18, 1776
C) September 15, 1780

544. How does Mrs. Allen know Mrs. Thorpe? (*Northanger Abbey*)

A) They are cousins.
B) Their parents were neighbors.
C) They attended boarding school together.

545. Who says this?
"I never wish to offend, but I am so foolishly shy, that I often seem negligent, when I am only kept back by my natural awkwardness."

A) Edmund Bertram (*Mansfield Park*)
B) Captain Wentworth (*Persuasion*)
C) Edward Ferrars (*Sense and Sensibility*)

546. Which character did Ciarán Hinds play in the 1995 movie version of *Persuasion*?

A) Mr. Elliot
B) Captain Wentworth
C) Charles Musgrove

547. What is the name of the Elizabeth Inchbald theatrical featured in *Mansfield Park*?

A) *The Wedding Day*
B) *To Marry, or not to Marry*
C) *Lovers' Vows*

548. Who says this?
"Oh! I am delighted with the book! I should like to spend my whole life in reading it."

A) Catherine Morland (*Northanger Abbey*)
B) Elizabeth Bennet (*Pride and Prejudice*)
C) Louisa Musgrove (*Persuasion*)

549. Which book does this quote come from?
"I would self-medicate with fat, carbohydrates, and Jane Austen, my number one drug of choice, my constant companion through every breakup, every disappointment, every crisis."

A) *Jane Austen: The Other Drug*
B) *Austenholics Anonymous*
C) *Confessions of a Jane Austen Addict*

550. How does Miss Bates know Jane Fairfax? (*Emma*)

A) Jane is her goddaughter.
B) Jane is her former pupil.
C) Jane is her niece.

551. Who says this to Edward Ferrars?

"Know your own happiness. You want nothing but patience--or give it a more fascinating name, call it hope." (*Sense and Sensibility*)

A) Mrs. Dashwood
B) Elinor Dashwood
C) Colonel Brandon

---

552. Which actor played Mr. Darcy in the 1940 MGM film version of *Pride and Prejudice*?

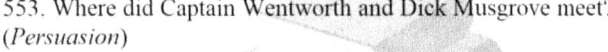

---

553. Where did Captain Wentworth and Dick Musgrove meet? (*Persuasion*)

A) Bath
B) Portsmouth
C) Gibraltor

---

554. Who says this?
"Miss Smith, indeed!--Oh! Miss Woodhouse! who can think of Miss Smith, when Miss Woodhouse is near!" (*Emma*)

A) Frank Churchill
B) Mr. Knightley
C) Mr. Elton

---

555. Where is Jane Austen buried?

A) Worcester Cathedral
B) Winchester Cathedral
C) Chichester Cathedral

556. Which castle does John Thorpe tell Catherine is "the finest place in England"?

A) Blaize Castle
B) Thornbury Castle
C) Farleigh Hungerford Castle

557. Who says this?
"Laugh as much as you chuse, but you will not laugh me out of my opinion." (*Pride and Prejudice*)

A) Jane Bennet
B) Charlotte Lucas
C) Mrs. Hurst

558. *The Trouble with Flirting* (2013, Claire LeZebnik) is a rewrite of which Austen novel?

A) *Emma*
B) *Mansfield Park*
C) *Pride and Prejudice*

559. What is the name of the property Lady Susan stopped her brother from purchasing? (*Lady Susan*)

A) Churchill
B) Vernon Castle
C) Parklands

560. Who says this?

"I suppose you know, ma'am, that Mr. Ferrars is married."

A) Mrs. Ferrars
B) Thomas
C) Colonel Brandon

561. Which of Jane Austen's novels was first accepted for publication, but was not published until much later?

A) *Pride and Prejudice*
B) *Sense and Sensibility*
C) *Northanger Abbey*

562. How many children does Jane watch in London? (*Pride and Prejudice*)

A) four
B) five
C) six

563. Which man does this refer to?
"The child was to be kept in bed and amused as quietly as possible; but what was there for a father to do? This was quite a female case, and it would be highly absurd in him."

A) Charles Musgrove (*Persuasion*)
B) Sir John Middleton (*Sense and Sensibility*)
C) John Knightley (*Emma*)

564. Whose body does Mr. Darcy get switched to in *Darcy by Any Other Name* (Laura Hile, 2016)?

A) Mr. Collins'
B) Mr. Bingley's
C) Mr. Wickham's

565. Which university does James Morland attend? (*Northanger Abbey*)

A) Cambridge
B) St. Andrews
C) Oxford

566. Who says this?
"I hate to hear you talk about all women as if they were fine ladies instead of rational creatures. None of us want to be in calm waters all our lives."

A) Elizabeth Bennet (*Pride and Prejudice*)
B) Sophia Croft (*Persuasion*)
C) Marianne Dashwood (*Sense and Sensibility*)

567. How old was Jane Austen when she died?

A) 37
B) 41
C) 43

568. What does Edmund Bertram bring to Fanny Price when she has "the headache"? (*Mansfield Park*)

A) aromatic vinegar
B) a hot water bottle
C) a glass of Madeira

569. Whom is being described?
"Her youth had passed without distinction, and her middle of life was devoted to the care of a failing mother and the endeavor to make a small income go as far as possible. And yet she was a happy woman."

A) Mrs. Price (*Mansfield Park*)
B) Mrs. Smith (*Persuasion*)
C) Miss Bates (*Emma*)

570. Which hero has Matthew Macfadyen played in an Austen-adapted movie?

A) Captain Wentworth
B) Mr. Darcy
C) Colonel Brandon

571. What is the name of the Dashwood's Sussex estate? (*Sense and Sensibility*)

A) Barton Park
B) Combe Magna
C) Norland Park

---

572. Whom is being described?
"[She] is the only one who has judged rightly throughout; who has been consistent. . . You will find [her] everything you could wish."

A) Fanny Price (*Mansfield Park*)
B) Elinor Dashwood (*Sense and Sensibility*)
C) Jane Bennet (*Pride and Prejudice*)

---

573. In which book does this appear?
"'If you ask me,' continued Flora, 'I think I have much in common with Miss Austen. She liked everything to be tidy and pleasant and comfortable around her, and so do I.'"

A) *I Captured the Castle*
B) *Cold Comfort Farm*
C) *Bridget Jones's Diary*

---

574. What is Mrs. Smith's maiden name? (*Persuasion*)

A) Hamilton
B) Young
C) Campbell

---

575. Whom is Elizabeth Bennet talking to?

"Your defect is a propensity to hate everybody." (*Pride and Prejudice*)

A) Catherine de Bourgh
B) Caroline Bingley
C) Mr. Darcy

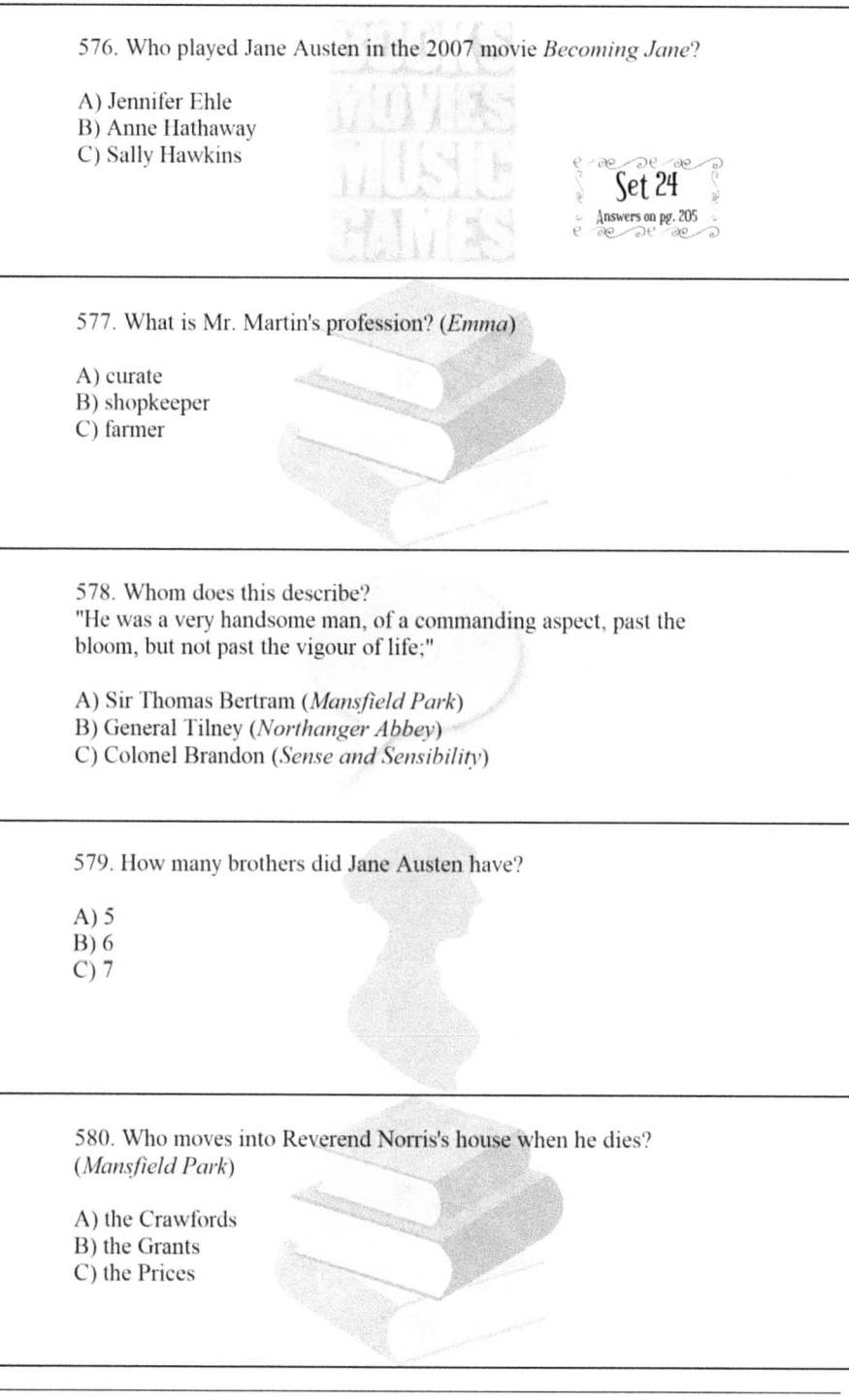

576. Who played Jane Austen in the 2007 movie *Becoming Jane*?

A) Jennifer Ehle
B) Anne Hathaway
C) Sally Hawkins

Set 24
Answers on pg. 205

577. What is Mr. Martin's profession? (*Emma*)

A) curate
B) shopkeeper
C) farmer

578. Whom does this describe?
"He was a very handsome man, of a commanding aspect, past the bloom, but not past the vigour of life;"

A) Sir Thomas Bertram (*Mansfield Park*)
B) General Tilney (*Northanger Abbey*)
C) Colonel Brandon (*Sense and Sensibility*)

579. How many brothers did Jane Austen have?

A) 5
B) 6
C) 7

580. Who moves into Reverend Norris's house when he dies?
(*Mansfield Park*)

A) the Crawfords
B) the Grants
C) the Prices

581. Whom does this describe?
"She had been forced into prudence in her youth, she learned romance as she grew older: the natural sequel of an unnatural beginning."

A) Elizabeth Bennet (*Pride and Prejudice*)
B) Elinor Dashwood (*Sense and Sensibility*)
C) Anne Elliot (*Persuasion*)

582. *The Dashwood Sisters Tell All* (Beth Pattillo, 2011) is a rewrite of which Jane Austen novel?

583. Who persuaded Anne Elliot to call off her engagement to Captain Wentworth in 1806? (*Persuasion*)

A) Sir Walter Elliot
B) Mrs. Clay
C) Lady Russell

584. Who says this?
"My dear Miss Elizabeth, I have the highest opinion in the world of your excellent judgment in all matters within the scope of your understanding . . ." (*Pride and Prejudice*)

A) Mr. Collins
B) Mr. Darcy
C) Mr. Wickham

585. It is possible Jane Austen originally intended *Persuasion* to be called _____.

A) *The Elliots*
B) *Second Chance*
C) *Reversal of Fortune*

586. Who pays for Jane Fairfax's education? (*Emma*)

A) Colonel Campbell
B) Mrs. Bates
C) Mr. Dixon

587. Who says this?
"I could not be happy with a man whose taste did not in every point coincide with my own. He must enter in all my feelings; the same books, the same music must charm us both."

A) Jane Bennet (*Pride and Prejudice*)
B) Mary Crawford (*Mansfield Park*)
C) Marianne Dashwood (*Sense and Sensibility*)

588. What is the title of the 2014 rewrite of *The Watsons* written by Ann Mychal?

A) *Emma and Elizabeth*
B) *Emma's Suitors*
C) *The Miss Watsons*

589. What are the opening words to *Mansfield Park*?

A) "About thirty years ago, Miss Maria Ward, of Huntingdon, with only seven thousand pounds. . ."
B) "The family of -------- had long been settled in Sussex. . ."
C) "No one who had ever seen [her] in her infancy would have supposed her born to be an heroine."

590. Mr. Knightley defines this word as having "English delicacy toward the feelings of other people." (*Emma*)

A) genteel
B) amiable
C) elegant

591. How old was Jane when she wrote *The History of England*?

A) 14
B) 15
C) 16

592. Where did the John Dashwoods reside in London? (*Sense and Sensibility*)

A) on Harley Street
B) on Wimpole Street
C) on Gracechurch Street

593. Who says this?
"Society has claims on us all; and I profess myself one of those who consider intervals of recreation and amusement as desirable for everybody." (*Pride and Prejudice*)

A) Mrs. Bennet
B) Mary Bennet
C) Kitty Bennet

594. What is the title of a Reginald Hill "completion" of *Sanditon* that renamed the resort "Sandytown" and placed it on the Yorkshire coast?

A) *The Price of Butcher's Meat*
B) *The Sandytown News*
C) *A Plate of Yorkshire Pudding*

595. Which book contains the following quote?
"But when a young lady is to be a heroine, the perverseness of forty surrounding families cannot prevent her. Something must and will happen to throw a hero in her way."

A) *Emma*
B) *Mansfield Park*
C) *Northanger Abbey*

596. Whom does this describe?
"[She, with] an elegance of mind and sweetness of character, which must have placed her high with any people of real understanding, was nobody with either father or sister."

A) Emma Woodhouse (*Emma*)
B) Anne Elliot (*Persuasion*)
C) Fanny Price (*Mansfield Park*)

597. Who said it?
"One of the reason's Jane Austen might not have married when she did have the opportunity...well, she watched her very dear nieces and friends die in childbirth!"

A) Veronica Roth
B) Suzanne Collins
C) Stephenie Meyer

598. Who has a baby in the course of the story? (*Emma*)

A) Mrs. Goddard
B) Mrs. Weston
C) Mrs. Elton

599. Whom does this describe?
"[She] was never satisfied with the day unless she spent the chief of it by the side of Mrs. Thorpe, . . . Mrs. Thorpe talked chiefly of her children, and [she] of her gowns." (*Northanger Abbey*)

A) Catherine Morland
B) Eleanor Tilney
C) Mrs. Allen

600. The Ash Grove Press published which version of *Pride and Prejudice*?

A) a children's book
B) a comic book
C) a board game

601. What is the "only ornament" that Fanny Price "ever had a desire to possess"? (*Mansfield Park*)

A) a cross
B) a gold chain
C) a bracelet

602. Whom is Mrs. Jennings talking to?
"[You] have taken Charlotte off my hands, and cannot give her back again." (*Sense and Sensibility*)

A) Mr. Palmer
B) Robert Ferrars
C) Sir John Middleton

603. Which novel was published along with *Persuasion* in a four-volume set after Jane Austen's death?

A) *Lady Susan*
B) *Northanger Abbey*
C) *Mansfield Park*

604. Whom does Lady Susan marry?

A) Sir James Martin
B) Mr. Manwaring
C) Reginald de Courcy

605. Whom does this describe?
"[Her] kindness extended farther than Elizabeth had any conception of; — its object was nothing else than to secure [Elizabeth] from any return of Mr. Collins's addresses, by engaging them towards herself." (*Pride and Prejudice*)

A) Mary Bennet
B) Charlotte Lucas
C) Jane Bennet

606. Who played Mr. Elton in the 1996 theatrical version of *Emma*?

A) Ewan McGregor
B) Jeremy Northam
C) Alan Cumming

607. What is the name of the vessel Captain Wentworth most recently commanded? (*Persuasion*)

A) the Laconia
B) the Asp
C) the Regis

608. Who says this?
"Oh for heaven's sake, are we to receive every Bennet in the country?"
(*Pride and Prejudice*)

A) Catherine de Bourgh
B) Sir William Lucas
C) Caroline Bingley

609. Where did Tom Lefroy, a love interest of Jane's, come from?

A) Scotland
B) Wales
C) Ireland

610. Who officially introduces Catherine Morland to Henry Tilney?
(*Northanger Abbey*)

A) Mr. King
B) General Courtenay
C) Captain Hunt

611. Whom does this describe?
"Angry she was: bitterly angry; but she was more angry with Fanny for having received such an offer than for refusing it. It was an injury and affront to Julia, who ought to have been Mr. Crawford's choice." (*Mansfield Park*)

A) Mrs. Norris
B) Lady Bertram
C) Mary Crawford

612. The Jane Austen Argument is a _____ .

A) literary forum
B) band
C) political movement

613. What is the name of Colonel Brandon's estate? (*Sense and Sensibility*)

A) Combe Magna
B) Delaford
C) Allenham

614. Whom is Mr. Knightley talking about?
"She has a fault. She has not the open temper which a man would wish for in a wife." (*Emma*)

A) Jane Fairfax
B) Harriet Smith
C) Augusta Elton

615. What did Jane Austen use as an "alarm" at Chawton Cottage to let her know someone was to disturb her writing?

A) a bell
B) a squeaky door
C) a parrot

616. What part in the play *Lovers' Vows* did each of the Bertram sisters feel a claim to? (*Mansfield Park*)

A) Agatha
B) Cottager's Wife
C) Amelia

617. Whom is Marianne Dashwood talking about?
"[H]e talked of flannel waistcoats. . . and with me a flannel waistcoat is invariably connected with the aches, cramps, rheumatisms, and every species of ailment that can afflict the old and the feeble." (*Sense and Sensibility*)

A) Sir John Middleton
B) Colonel Brandon
C) Mr. Palmer

618. What is the name of an updated version of *Persuasion* by Kaitlin Saunders (2011)?

A) *Anne, Persuaded*
B) *A Modern Day Persuasion*
C) *Remembrance and Regret*

619. Mrs. Bennet is proud of the fact her daughters do not need to _____. (*Pride and Prejudice*)

A) get an education
B) cook
C) do needlework

620. Whom does this describe?
"Catherine's silent appeal to her friend, meanwhile, was entirely thrown away, for [she], not being at all in the habit of conveying any expression herself by a look, was not aware of its being ever intended by anybody else." (*Northanger Abbey*)

A) Miss Tilney
B) Isabella Thorpe
C) Mrs. Allen

621. "One doesn't read Jane Austen; one _____ Jane Austen." (William F. Buckley, Jr.)

A) savors
B) re-reads
C) falls in love with

622. What is the "misfortune, which about this time befell Mrs. John Dashwood"? (*Sense and Sensibility*)

A) finding out about the engagement between Lucy Steele and Edward Ferrars
B) having a friend suspect her of housing the Dashwood girls
C) being required to admire Elinor's screens

623. Whom is Elizabeth Bennet talking about?
"I cannot make him out. There is something very pompous in his style. — And what can he mean by apologizing for being next in the entail? — We cannot suppose he would help it if he could." (*Pride and Prejudice*)

A) Colonel Fitzwilliam
B) Mr. Darcy
C) Mr. Collins

624. *Mount Hope* (2016, Sarah Price) is an Amish rewrite of which Austen novel?

A) *Northanger Abbey*
B) *Mansfield Park*
C) *Pride and Prejudice*

625. Who works land that Mr. Knightley owns? (*Emma*)

A) Frank Churchill
B) Mr. Weston
C) Robert Martin

626. Who says this?
"I do not think I ever opened a book in my life which had not something to say upon woman's inconstancy. Songs and proverbs, all talk of woman's fickleness."

A) Frank Churchill (*Emma*)
B) Captain Harville (*Persuasion*)
C) Robert Ferrars (*Sense and Sensibility*)

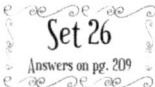

627. Which estate is featured on the £10 note along with Jane Austen's likeness?

A) Chawton Cottage
B) Godmersham Park
C) Steventon Rectory

628. Which of these books did Jane Austen quit writing at chapter 12?

A) *Sanditon*
B) *The Watsons*
C) *Lady Susan*

629. Who says this?
"I pay very little regard to what any person says on the subject of marriage. If they profess a disinclination for it, I only set it down that they have not yet seen the right person."

A) Lady Russell (*Persuasion*)
B) Mrs. Jennings (*Sense and Sensibility*)
C) Mrs. Grant (*Mansfield Park*)

630. What is the name of a novel adaptation of *Pride and Prejudice* that features Elizabeth Bennet as a spirit?

A) *Pride and Paranormal*
B) *Elizabeth Bennet's Afterlife*
C) *Haunting Mr. Darcy*

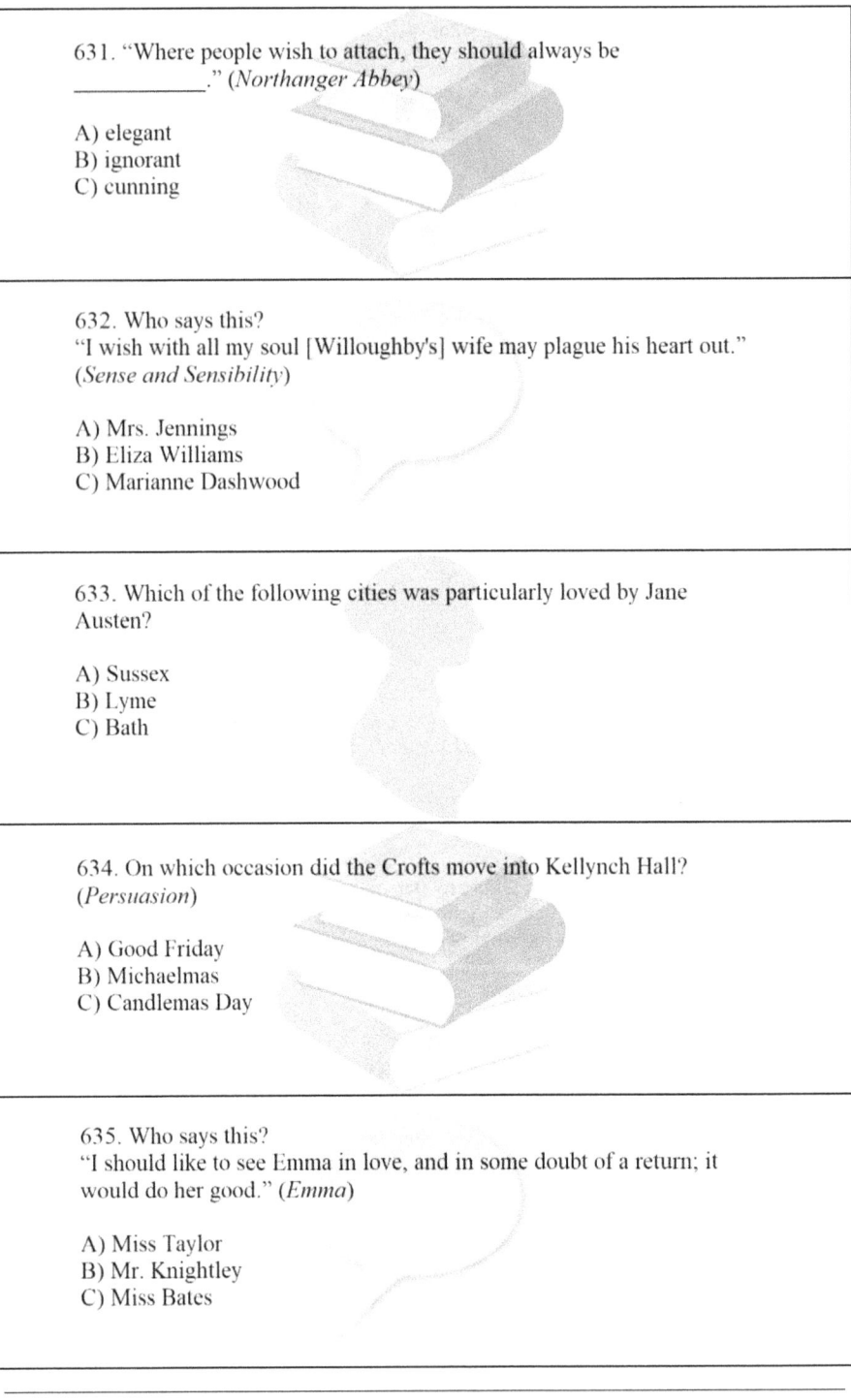

631. "Where people wish to attach, they should always be
_____." (*Northanger Abbey*)

A) elegant
B) ignorant
C) cunning

632. Who says this?
"I wish with all my soul [Willoughby's] wife may plague his heart out."
(*Sense and Sensibility*)

A) Mrs. Jennings
B) Eliza Williams
C) Marianne Dashwood

633. Which of the following cities was particularly loved by Jane
Austen?

A) Sussex
B) Lyme
C) Bath

634. On which occasion did the Crofts move into Kellynch Hall?
(*Persuasion*)

A) Good Friday
B) Michaelmas
C) Candlemas Day

635. Who says this?
"I should like to see Emma in love, and in some doubt of a return; it
would do her good." (*Emma*)

A) Miss Taylor
B) Mr. Knightley
C) Miss Bates

636. What is the title of a novel of Jane Austen's life, written by Syrie James (2009)?

A) *The Lost Memoirs of Jane Austen*
B) *Jane Austen's Romance*
C) *Jane Austen Remembers*

637. What is Sam Watson's profession? (*The Watsons*)

A) factory owner
B) surgeon
C) gentleman

638. Who says this?
"When I look out on such a night as this, I feel as if there could be neither wickedness nor sorrow in the world; and there certainly would be less of both if the sublimity of nature were more attended to."

A) Marianne Dashwood (*Sense and Sensibility*)
B) Elizabeth Bennet (*Pride and Prejudice*)
C) Fanny Price (*Mansfield Park*)

639. Which university were women allowed to attend in Jane Austen's day?

A) Oxford
B) Cambridge
C) Edinburgh University
D) None of the above

640. Whom does Caroline hope her brother will marry? (*Pride and Prejudice*)

A) Jane Bennet
B) Georgiana Darcy
C) Charlotte Lucas

641. What is Mrs. Dashwood talking about?
"I have not wanted syllables where actions have spoken so plainly."
(*Sense and Sensibility*)

A) Marianne and Willoughby's engagement
B) Elinor and Edward's engagement
C) Lucy and Edward's engagement

642. What is "The Jane Austen Drinking Game"?

A) a radio skit
B) a card game
C) a chapter from a book

643. Who tells Captain Wentworth she wishes Charles would have married Anne instead of Mary? (*Persuasion*)

A) Elizabeth Elliot
B) Louisa Musgrove
C) Mrs. Smith

644. Whom does this describe?
"What was unwholesome to him he regarded as unfit for anybody; and he had, therefore, earnestly tried to dissuade them from having any wedding-cake, at all."

A) Mr. Collins (*Pride and Prejudice*)
B) Mr. Allen (*Northanger Abbey*)
C) Mr. Woodhouse (*Emma*)

645. Who said it?
"I like [Austen's Elinor Dashwood] but I can see how she would drive you mad. She's just the sort of person you'd want to get drunk, just to make her giggling and silly."

A) Kate Winslet
B) Hugh Grant
C) Emma Thompson

646. What was Catherine's favorite game when she was a child? (*Northanger Abbey*)

A) cricket
B) whist
C) blind man's bluff

647. Who says this?
"A sailor grows old sooner than any other man. I have observed it all my life. A man is in greater danger in the navy of . . . becoming prematurely an object of disgust himself, than in any other line." (*Persuasion*)

A) Captain Harville
B) Admiral Croft
C) Sir Walter Elliot

648. What is the name of a "sequel" to *Pride and Prejudice* written by Jennifer Paynter (2014) that focuses on Mary Bennet?

A) *Mary's Chance*
B) *The Forgotten Sister*
C) *The Unlikely Sister*

649. What puzzled Mary Crawford about Fanny Price soon after she became acquainted with the family? (*Mansfield Park*)

A) Whether she was related to the Bertrams.
B) Whether she was musical or artistic.
C) Whether she was "out."

650. Whom does this describe?
". . .the very gentleman whose negligent servant left behind him that collection of washing-bills, resulting from a long visit at Northanger, by which my heroine was involved in one of her most alarming adventures."

A) the viscount Miss Tilney marries
B) Captain Tilney
C) John Thorpe

651. Jane Austen was the _____ child in her family.

A) 4th
B) 5th
C) 7th

Set 27
Answers on pg. 211

652. Which place has "dark narrow stairs and a kitchen that smokes"? (*Sense and Sensibility*)

A) The Crown Inn
B) Allenham
C) Barton Cottage

653. Whom does this describe?
"[He] was the happy man towards whom almost every female eye was turned, and Elizabeth was the happy woman by whom he finally seated himself." (*Pride and Prejudice*)

A) Mr. Wickham
B) Mr. Darcy
C) Mr. Bingley

654. Who played Captain Wentworth in the TV series adaptation of *Persuasion* in 1971?

A) Peter Firth
B) Bryan Marshall
C) David Rintoul

655. What is Mrs. Elton's maiden name? (*Emma*)

A) Hawkins
B) Suckling
C) Partridge

656. Whom does this describe?

"[He] was a young man of good abilities, quick imagination, lively spirits, and open, affectionate manners. He was exactly formed to engage Marianne's heart." (*Sense and Sensibility*)

657. Which language was considered a "man's" language and was not usually taught to women in Jane's day?

A) Italian
B) Greek
C) French

658. Whom is the first person Elizabeth sees after learning of Lydia's elopement? (*Pride and Prejudice*)

A) Mr. Darcy
B) Mr. Gardiner
C) Mr. Wickham

659. Who says this?
"An agreeable manner may set off handsome features, but can never alter plain ones." (*Persuasion*)

A) Mrs. Clay
B) Elizabeth Elliot
C) Henrietta Musgrove

660. What is the name of Debra White Smith's modern adaptation of *Mansfield Park*?

A) *A Visit to Mansfield*
B) *A Park to Remember*
C) *Central Park*

661. How many children do the Heywoods have?
(*Sanditon*)

A) 8
B) 11
C) 14

662. Which heroine does this describe?
"Her heart did whisper that he had done it for her."

A) Elizabeth Bennet (*Pride and Prejudice*)
B) Anne Elliot (*Persuasion*)
C) Elinor Dashwood (*Sense and Sensibility*)

663. Which of the following was NOT considered an acceptable
gentlewoman's "accomplishment" in Jane's day?

A) drawing
B) cooking
C) music
D) dancing

664. Who taught French to Catherine? (*Northanger Abbey*)

A) Mrs. Allen
B) a tutor
C) her mother

665. Whom does this describe?
"[She] was the mistress of a school – . . .a real, honest, old-fashioned
boarding school."

A) Mrs. Rushworth (*Mansfield Park*)
B) Mrs. Clay (*Persuasion*)
C) Mrs. Goddard (*Emma*)

666. Who played Elinor Dashwood in the 1971 film version of *Sense and Sensibility*?

A) Ciaran Madden
B) Joanna David
C) Irene Richards

667. What is Captain Benwick's favorite topic of discussion with Anne Elliot? (*Persuasion*)

A) his travels
B) poetry
C) history

668. Which word fills in the blank?
"Oh! Do not attack me with your _____." (Mary Crawford, *Mansfield Park*)

A) watch
B) opinion
C) pen

669. Who said it?
"[Jane Austen] has compelled the amazed admiration of writers of the most diverse kinds."

A) Edmund Wilson
B) John Peale Bishop
C) Allen Tate

670. What is the name of the governess who assists Wickham in his schemes? (*Pride and Prejudice*)

A) Mrs. Hurst
B) Mrs. Younge
C) Mrs. Phillips

671. Whom is Marianne talking about?
"To say that he is unlike Fanny is enough. It implies everything amiable. I love him already." (*Sense and Sensibility*)

A) Mr. Willoughby
B) Edward Ferrars
C) Colonel Brandon

672. What is the name of a 2007 drama starring Olivia Williams as Jane Austen?

A) *Becoming Jane*
B) *Miss Austen Regrets*
C) *Jane Austen Country*

673. What is Miss Bates' first name? (*Emma*)

A) Isabella
B) Anna
C) Hetty

674. What was Catherine Morland referring to (though she didn't know it at the time) when she said this?
"I have heard that something very shocking indeed will soon come out of London." (*Northanger Abbey*)

A) murder
B) a new publication
C) a riot

675. What is Jane Austen's mother's name?

A) Elizabeth
B) Cassandra
C) Catherine

676. What does Mrs. Norris stipulate that Fanny could never have in the East Room on her own account? (*Mansfield Park*)

A) books
B) plants
C) a fire

677. Whom does this describe?
"When lovely woman stoops to folly, she has nothing to do but to die; and when she stoops to be disagreeable, it is equally recommended as a clearer of ill fame." (*Emma*)

A) Mrs. Woodhouse
B) Mrs. Weston
C) Mrs. Churchill

678. Which airline put Jane Austen's face on their planes' tail fins in 2018?

A) Norwegian
B) British Airways
C) Ryanair

679. How are Marianne and Elinor Dashwood related to John Dashwood? (*Sense and Sensibility*)

A) They are cousins.
B) They are his sisters.
C) They are his half-sisters.

680. Whom does this describe?
"[She is] so plain and awkward, that she would never have been tolerated in Camden-place but for her birth."

A) Miss Cartaret (*Persuasion*)
B) Mary Bennet (*Pride and Prejudice*)
C) Miss Morton (*Sense and Sensibility*)

681. Which of Jane's brothers taught her about life in the British navy—knowledge she used in *Persuasion*?

A) James
B) Frank
C) Henry

682. How long did Catherine study the spinnet? (*Northanger Abbey*)

A) two months
B) one year
C) four years

683. Whom is Charlotte talking about?
"He is so droll! . . . He is always out of humor." (*Sense and Sensibility*)

A) Colonel Brandon
B) Mr. Palmer
C) Sir John Middleton

684. What is the name of a TV series involving a girl who runs the matchmaking and lifestyle division of Highbury Partners Lifestyle?

A) *Emma's Advice*
B) *Dear Emma*
C) *Emma Approved*

685. How old was Fanny Price when she was sent to live with the Bertrams? (*Mansfield Park*)

A) ten
B) eleven
C) twelve

686. Whom is Mrs. Hurst talking about?
"I shall never forget her appearance this morning. She looked almost wild... I hope you saw her petticoat, six inches deep in mud." (*Pride and Prejudice*)

A) Elizabeth Bennet
B) Mary Bennet
C) Jane Bennet

687. Which novel was Jane writing when she died?

A) *Northanger Abbey*
B) *Sanditon*
C) *The Watsons*

688. Who believes her daughter would be wasting time by learning languages, music, and drawing?

A) Lady Catherine de Bourgh (*Pride and Prejudice*)
B) Mrs. Thorpe (*Northanger Abbey*)
C) Lady Susan Vernon (*Lady Susan*)

689. Who says this to Catherine Morland?
"Yes, I know exactly what [your journal] will say: Friday, went to the Lower Rooms; wore my sprigged muslin robe with blue trimmings – plain black shoes – appeared to much advantage." (*Northanger Abbey*)

A) John Thorpe
B) Henry Tilney
C) James Morland

690. What is the title of a book that summarizes *Pride and Prejudice* as "Girl hates wealthy aristocrat. Wait, no she doesn't."?

A) *CliffsNotes of CliffsNotes*
B) *Swift Summaries of Classic Books*
C) *Abridged Classics*

691. Where does "Catherine, or the Bower" appear?

A) *Juvenilia*
B) *The Watsons*
C) *Sanditon*

---

692. Whom is Mrs. Smith talking about?
"[She is a] shrewd, intelligent, sensible woman." (*Persuasion*)

A) Elizabeth Elliot
B) Mrs. Clay
C) Nurse Rooke

---

693. Who said it?
"The key to Jane Austen's fortune with posterity has been in part the extraordinary grace of her facility... little master-strokes of imagination."

A) James Joyce
B) Nathaniel Hawthorne
C) Henry James

---

694. How many false engagements were suspected in *Sense and Sensibility*?

---

695. Whom does this describe?
"[He] now received his daughter; and having. . . observed that she was grown into a woman, and he supposed would be wanting a husband soon, seemed very much inclined to forget her again."
(*Mansfield Park*)

A) Mr. Price
B) Thomas Bertram
C) Dr. Grant

696. *Ruby in Paradise* (1993) is a movie homage to which Jane Austen novel?

A) *Persuasion*
B) *Mansfield Park*
C) *Northanger Abbey*

697. Whom does Lady Susan want her daughter to marry?

A) Sir James Martin
B) Reginald de Courcy
C) Charles Smith

698. Whom does this describe?
"She meant to shine and be very superior, but with manners which had been formed in a bad school, pert and familiar; that all her notions were drawn from one set of people, and one style of living."

A) Mrs. Elton (*Emma*)
B) Lady Bertram (*Mansfield Park*)
C) Charlotte Palmer (*Sense and Sensibility*)

699. What happened to prevent Jane's again meeting with a young clergyman she'd fallen for in 1801?

A) he was sent abroad
B) he died
C) he got engaged to someone else

700. What is Mr. Gardiner's occupation? (*Pride and Prejudice*)

A) merchant
B) officer
C) clergyman

701. What is the name of the uncle Lucy Steele is talking about?
"[Edward Ferrars] was four years with my uncle, who lives at
Longstaple, near Plymouth. . . it was there our engagement was formed."
(*Sense and Sensibility*)

A) John Middleton
B) Mr. Pratt
C) Lord Morton

Set 29
Answers on pg. 215

702. *Trishna* (1985) is an Indian TV series adaptation of which Jane
Austen novel?

A) *Pride and Prejudice*
B) *Sense and Sensibility*
C) *Emma*

703. What Shakespeare play does Henry Crawford start reading,
captivating Fanny Price against her will? (*Mansfield Park*)

A) *Henry the Eighth*
B) *Othello*
C) *Hamlet*

704. Whom does this describe?
"[They] had had the ill fortune of a very troublesome, hopeless son; and
the good fortune to lose him before he reach[ed] his twentieth year."

A) Mr. and Mrs. Musgrove (*Persuasion*)
B) Mr. and Mrs. Price (*Mansfield Park*)
C) Mr. and Mrs. Morland (*Northanger Abbey*)

705. Which phrase, used in *Mansfield Park*, did Jane Austen use for
the first time in literature?

A) "evening party"
B) "dinner party"
C) "garden party"

706. Which kind of dog does Henry Tilney have? (*Northanger Abbey*)

A) Newfoundland
B) Spaniel
C) Corgi

707. Whom is Jane Bennet talking about?
"When she did come, it was very evident that she had no pleasure in it; she made a slight, formal apology for not calling before, said not a word of wishing to see me again, and was in every respect [an altered] creature. . ." (*Pride and Prejudice*)

A) Catherine de Bourgh
B) Caroline Bingley
C) Mrs. Gardiner

708. What is the name of a 1980 movie, concerning stage adaptations of an early Jane Austen work, starring Anne Baxter?

A) *Jane Austen Takes Center Stage*
B) *Jane Austen's Green Room*
C) *Jane Austen in Manhattan*

709. What does Henry Dashwood get his son John to promise him before his death? (*Sense and Sensibility*)

A) That he will never sell Norland Park.
B) That he will help his 2nd wife and her children.
C) That he will educate his son properly.

710. Whom was Catherine Morland talking about?

"When she first knew what my father would do for them, she seemed quite disappointed that it was not more. I never was so deceived in anyone's character in my life before." (*Northanger Abbey*)

711. What "business" did Jane's father run out of their home?

A) a tea shop
B) a school for boys
C) a tailor shop

712. What did Mr. Elliot previously study before his marriage? (*Persuasion*)

A) politics
B) business
C) law

713. Whom does this describe?
"There were none within the circle of her father's and mother's acquaintance to afford her the smallest satisfaction: she saw nobody in whose favour she could wish to overcome her own shyness and reserve."

A) Fanny Price (*Mansfield Park*)
B) Jane Bennet (*Pride and Prejudice*)
C) Elinor Dashwood (*Sense and Sensibility*)

714. Which adaptation has Lizzy Bennet and George Wickham connect as childhood friends?

A) *A Good Name* (Sarah Courtney)
B) *Undoing* (L.L. Diamond)
C) *Only the Deepest Love* (Amelia Wood)

715. Which character in *Sanditon* CANNOT be considered a "hypochondriac"?

A) Sidney Parker
B) Susan Parker
C) Diana Parker

716. Who says this?
"If I had ever learnt [the piano], I should have been a great proficient."

A) Lady Bertram (*Mansfield Park*)
B) Mrs. Jennings (*Sense and Sensibility*)
C) Catherine de Bourgh (*Pride and Prejudice*)

---

717. Who said it?
"Jane Austen, of course, wise in her neatness, trim in her sedateness; she never fails, but there are few or none like her."

A) Edith Wharton
B) Kate Chopin
C) Charlotte Perkins Gilman

---

718. How many shillings does Henry mention paying for muslin? (*Northanger Abbey*)

A) five
B) seven
C) eight

---

719. Whom does this describe?
"She could not but in conscience feel that [this family] were gone who deserved not to stay, and that Kellynch-hall had passed into better hands than its owners." (*Persuasion*)

A) Sophia Croft
B) Anne Elliot
C) Lady Russell

---

720. *Metropolitan* (1990) is a loose movie adaptation of which novel?

A) *Mansfield Park*
B) *Persuasion*
C) *Emma*

721. Mrs. Dashwood and daughters move from Sussex to which county? (*Sense and Sensibility*)

A) Derbyshire
B) Dorsetshire
C) Devonshire

722. Whom does this describe?
"His cousin Charles Hayter was an eldest son, and he saw things as an eldest son himself."

A) Charles Musgrove (*Persuasion*)
B) Edward Ferrars (*Sense and Sensibility*)
C) Mr. Bingley (*Pride and Prejudice*)

723. Which disease nearly took Jane Austen's life in her youth?

A) typhus
B) cholera
C) scarlet fever

724. How many times is Emma proposed to? (*Emma*)

A) once
B) twice
C) three times

725. Whom does this describe?
"[She] saw that much was wrong at home, and wanted to set it right. . . Fanny soon became more disposed to admire the natural light of [her] mind which could so early distinguish justly." (*Mansfield Park*)

A) Susan Price
B) Betsey Price
C) Mrs. Price

726. What is the name of a collection of stories (2011) inspired by Jane Austen's works?

A) *What Would Jane Do?*
B) *Born an Heroine*
C) *Jane Austen Made Me Do It*

Set 30
Answers on pg. 217

727. Where do Catherine, Henry and Eleanor go for a walk in the countryside? (*Northanger Abbey*)

A) Beechen Cliff
B) around Northanger Abbey
C) near an old Gothic church

728. Who said it?
"You may believe me. I never compliment."

A) Mr. Darcy (*Pride and Prejudice*)
B) Mrs. Ferrars (*Sense and Sensibility*)
C) Mrs. Elton (*Emma*)

729. What was the name of the Frances Burney book that inspired the title *Pride and Prejudice*?

A) *Cecilia*
B) *Camilla*
C) *Evelina*

730. Which of the following did not know of Anne's previous engagement to Captain Wentworth? (*Persuasion*)

A) Elizabeth Elliot
B) Mary Musgrove
C) Lady Russell

731. Whom is Elinor talking to?
"Engaged to Mr. Edward Ferrars! . . but surely there must be some mistake of person or name. We cannot mean the same Mr. Ferrars."
(*Sense and Sensibility*)

A) Marianne Dashwood
B) Lucy Steele
C) Miss Morton

---

732. What is the title of a modern version of *Pride and Prejudice* in which Elizabeth is a celebrity chef (2014)?

A) *The Bennet Buffet*
B) *Lizzy and Jane*
C) *Pie and Prejudice*

---

733. What was Fanny Price "rhapsodising" about while sitting out of doors with Mary Crawford? (*Mansfield Park*)

A) the fine autumn day
B) different kinds of friendship
C) the evergreen

---

734. Who says this?
"I will not allow it to be more man's nature than woman's to be inconstant and forget those they do love, or have loved. I believe the reverse."

A) Captain Harville (*Persuasion*)
B) Edward Ferrars (*Sense and Sensibility*)
C) Mr. Knightley (*Emma*)

---

735. Who is the person that was suprisingly mentioned in Jane Austen's will?

A) her childhood friend
B) her dead aunt
C) her brother's secretary

736. What did Willoughby give to Marianne as a gift? (*Sense and Sensibility*)

A) a lock of his hair
B) a horse
C) a book about wild flowers

737. Whom does this describe?
"There is no danger of Wickham's marrying [her]. . . She is gone down to her uncle at Liverpool: gone to stay." (*Pride and Prejudice*)

A) Lydia Bennet
B) Georgiana Darcy
C) Mary King

738. What is the name of a 2006 stage play about Jane Austen's choices in her love life?

A) *Jane, the Musical*
B) *Jane's Lost Love*
C) *In Want of a Husband*

739. Which novel does the following passage come from?
"And if the distress be not poignant enough to keep the eyes unclosed, they will be sure to open to sensations of softened pain and brighter hope."

A) *Mansfield Park*
B) *Persuasion*
C) *Emma*

740. Whom is Mr. Willoughby talking about?
"There are some people who cannot bear a party of pleasure. [He] is one of them. He was afraid of catching cold I dare say, and invented this trick for getting out of it." (*Sense and Sensibility*)

A) Edward Ferrars
B) John Middleton
C) Colonel Brandon

741. Who said it?
"Just the omission of Jane Austen's books alone would make a fairly good library out of a library that hadn't a book in it."

A) Edgar Allan Poe
B) Mark Twain
C) John Steinbeck

742. What is the name of Captain Wentworth's brother? (*Persuasion*)

A) James
B) Richard
C) Edward

743. Whom does this describe?
"It often grieved [Fanny] to the heart to think . . .that [this woman], as handsome as Lady Bertram, and some years her junior, should have an appearance so much more worn and faded, so comfortless, so slatternly, so shabby." (*Mansfield Park*)

A) Mrs. Rushworth
B) Mrs. Norris
C) Mrs. Price

744. Which actress played both Elizabeth Bennet and Anne Elliot in different TV series?

A) Daphne Slater
B) Jane Downs
C) Ann Firbank

745. What is the name of the Vernon's estate? (*Lady Susan*)

A) Churchill
B) Parklands
C) Langford

746. Whom does this describe?
"[She] was deeply mortified by Darcy's marriage." (*Pride and Prejudice*)

A) Anne de Bourgh
B) Caroline Bingley
C) Charlotte Lucas

747. What is Jane Austen's mother's maiden name?

A) Leigh
B) Knight
C) Hampson

748. What does John Dashwood plan to build "upon the knoll behind the house"? (*Sense and Sensibility*)

A) a Grecian Temple
B) a green-house
C) a gazebo

749. Who says this?
"A man. . .must have a very good opinion of himself when he asks people to leave their own fireside, and encounter such a day as this, for the sake of coming to see him . . . It is the greatest absurdity." (*Emma*)

A) John Knightley
B) Frank Churchill
C) Mr. Elton

750. What is the name of a radio sitcom in which Jane Austen is a character in Hell?

A) *Births, Deaths, and Marriages*
B) *Ladies of Letters*
C) *Old Harry's Game*

Answers

Set 1	
1.	Bath
2.	A
3.	B
4.	C
5.	C
6.	A
7.	A
8.	B
9.	breakfast
10.	B
11.	A
12.	C
13.	C
14.	B
15.	A
16.	C
17.	A
18.	C
19.	B
20.	B
21.	C
22.	B
23.	C
24.	A
25.	A

Set 2	
26.	B
27.	A
28.	C
29.	C
30.	B
31.	B
32.	C
33.	C
34.	A
35.	A
36.	*Bride and Prejudice (2004)*
37.	B
38.	C
39.	B
40.	A
41.	C
42.	Ang Lee
43.	B
44.	B
45.	B
46.	C
47.	A
48.	B
49.	in want of a wife
50.	B

Set 3	
51.	A
52.	B
53.	C
54.	A
55.	B
56.	A
57.	B
58.	C
59.	C
60.	B
61.	C
62.	A
63.	C
64.	B
65.	C
66.	A
67.	C
68.	C
69.	C
70.	A
71.	A
72.	C
73.	B
74.	C
75.	C

Set 4	
76.	A
77.	A
78.	A
79.	B
80.	C
81.	B
82.	B
83.	A
84.	C
85.	She's Mrs. Bennet's sister.
86.	B
87.	C
88.	C
89.	B
90.	B
91.	A
92.	B
93.	C
94.	A
95.	A
96.	B
97.	B
98.	B
99.	C
100.	A

Set 5	
101.	A
102.	A
103.	False (It was Bath.)
104.	C
105.	B
106.	A
107.	B
108.	C
109.	B
110.	B
111.	B
112.	A
113.	C
114.	*P&P* (It was called *Miss Elizabeth Bennet*.)
115.	C
116.	C
117.	B
118.	A
119.	A
120.	B
121.	A
122.	A
123.	C
124.	C
125.	B

Set 6	
126.	B
127.	False
128.	B
129.	C
130.	B
131.	A
132.	A
133.	A
134.	C
135.	B
136.	B
137.	B
138.	*Pride and Prejudice and Zombies*
139.	A
140.	A
141.	C
142.	B
143.	Mr. Darcy
144.	B
145.	C
146.	B
147.	True
148.	B
149.	A
150.	C

Set 7	
151.	C
152.	B
153.	A
154.	B
155.	A
156.	B
157.	A
158.	B
159.	A
160.	C
161.	A
162.	C
163.	C
164.	B
165.	Janeite
166.	B
167.	B
168.	C
169.	A
170.	B
171.	St. Michael's Day, Sept 29th
172.	B
173.	C
174.	C
175.	A

Set 8	
176.	B
177.	A
178.	B
179.	A
180.	A
181.	B
182.	B
183.	True
184.	C
185.	A
186.	Hugh Grant
187.	C
188.	A
189.	C
190.	C
191.	A
192.	B
193.	Her sister married his brother.
194.	A
195.	A
196.	C
197.	C
198.	B
199.	A
200.	C

Set 9	
201.	C
202.	A
203.	A
204.	A
205.	B
206.	B
207.	B
208.	A
209.	C
210.	A
211.	False
212.	A
213.	B
214.	A
215.	B
216.	A
217.	B
218.	C
219.	clergyman
220.	A
221.	A
222.	C
223.	C
224.	B
225.	False (He would never smoke in front of a lady.)

Set 10	
226.	B
227.	A
228.	A
229.	A
230.	C
231.	False (They could only dance twice.)
232.	B
233.	B
234.	A
235.	A
236.	A
237.	B
238.	A
239.	C
240.	B
241.	C
242.	C
243.	A
244.	C
245.	A
246.	B
247.	B
248.	C
249.	A
250.	A

Set 11	
251.	A
252.	C
253.	A
254.	A
255.	C
256.	C
257.	B
258.	A
259.	B
260.	A
261.	B
262.	B
263.	C
264.	A
265.	A
266.	C
267.	B
268.	C
269.	B
270.	*Pride and Prejudice*
271.	B
272.	A
273.	C
274.	B
275.	C

Set 12	
276.	A
277.	B
278.	B
279.	The Jane Austen Society of North America
280.	A
281.	C
282.	A
283.	B
284.	C
285.	B
286.	C
287.	B
288.	A
289.	C
290.	A
291.	B
292.	C
293.	C
294.	A
295.	C
296.	B
297.	B
298.	A
299.	B
300.	B

Set 13	
301.	C
302.	Elizabeth Bennet
303.	A
304.	C
305.	A
306.	C
307.	A
308.	A
309.	B
310.	B
311.	C
312.	*Bridget Jones's Diary*
313.	C
314.	A
315.	*Emma*
316.	B
317.	Jane Bennet
318.	A
319.	C
320.	C
321.	A
322.	B
323.	C
324.	True
325.	C

Set 14

326.	A
327.	Gretna Green
328.	A
329.	A
330.	B
331.	C
332.	A
333.	C
334.	C
335.	B
336.	B
337.	A
338.	A
339.	False (They did not kiss.)
340.	B
341.	B
342.	C
343.	A
344.	A
345.	B
346.	A
347.	C
348.	C
349.	A
350.	B

Set 15	
351.	A
352.	B
353.	B
354.	C
355.	B
356.	C
357.	C
358.	B
359.	C
360.	A
361.	A
362.	B
363.	A
364.	C
365.	A
366.	B
367.	C
368.	A
369.	C
370.	C
371.	B
372.	C
373.	C
374.	A
375.	A

Set 16

376.	B
377.	B
378.	B
379.	C
380.	B
381.	A
382.	B
383.	A
384.	C
385.	C
386.	Catherine Morland
387.	C
388.	B
389.	C
390.	B
391.	A
392.	B
393.	*Emma*
394.	B
395.	C
396.	C
397.	B
398.	B
399.	False (It was her sister, Cassandra.)
400.	C

Set 17	
401.	C
402.	Andrew Davies' (1995 version)
403.	B
404.	A
405.	A
406.	B
407.	A
408.	B
409.	C
410.	C
411.	A
412.	B
413.	C
414.	B
415.	B
416.	A
417.	A
418.	C
419.	B
420.	A
421.	A
422.	C
423.	A
424.	B
425.	C

Set 18	
426.	A
427.	B
428.	A
429.	B
430.	B
431.	A
432.	B
433.	C
434.	B
435.	A
436.	C
437.	C
438.	A
439.	A
440.	Marianne Dashwood
441.	C
442.	A
443.	A
444.	C
445.	C
446.	A
447.	A
448.	B
449.	C
450.	B

Set 19

451.	C
452.	C
453.	B
454.	C
455.	B
456.	B
457.	A
458.	A
459.	Elizabeth Bennet
460.	C
461.	A
462.	Gwyneth Paltrow
463.	A
464.	C
465.	A
466.	C
467.	B
468.	B
469.	C
470.	C
471.	A
472.	B
473.	C
474.	B
475.	B

Set 20	
476.	C
477.	A
478.	A
479.	A
480.	B
481.	C
482.	C
483.	False (They didn't talk to or about the servants.)
484.	C
485.	A
486.	C
487.	B
488.	B
489.	True
490.	C
491.	C
492.	B
493.	C
494.	A
495.	False
496.	A
497.	B
498.	C
499.	C
500.	A

Set 21	
501.	C
502.	D
503.	C
504.	B
505.	B
506.	C
507.	The piano
508.	C
509.	A
510.	*Pride and Prejudice*
511.	C
512.	C
513.	A
514.	B
515.	A
516.	A
517.	B
518.	A
519.	*Fordyce's Sermons*
520.	A
521.	A
522.	B
523.	B
524.	A
525.	A

Set 22

526.	B
527.	C
528.	A
529.	B
530.	C
531.	A
532.	C
533.	A
534.	B
535.	A
536.	A
537.	False (Only women wore them.)
538.	B
539.	B
540.	A
541.	A
542.	B
543.	A
544.	C
545.	C
546.	B
547.	C
548.	A
549.	C
550.	C

Set 23	
551.	A
552.	Laurence Olivier
553.	C
554.	C
555.	B
556.	A
557.	A
558.	B
559.	B
560.	B
561.	C
562.	A
563.	A
564.	A
565.	C
566.	B
567.	B
568.	C
569.	C
570.	B
571.	C
572.	A
573.	B
574.	A
575.	C

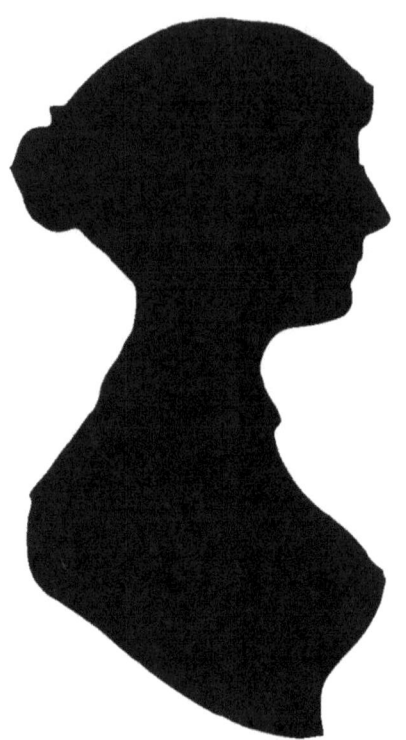

Set 24	
576.	B
577.	C
578.	B
579.	B
580.	B
581.	C
582.	*Sense & Sensibility*
583.	C
584.	A
585.	A
586.	A
587.	C
588.	A
589.	A
590.	B
591.	B
592.	A
593.	B
594.	A
595.	C
596.	B
597.	C
598.	B
599.	C
600.	C

Set 25

601.	B
602.	A
603.	B
604.	A
605.	B
606.	C
607.	A
608.	C
609.	C
610.	A
611.	A
612.	B
613.	B
614.	A
615.	B
616.	A
617.	B
618.	B
619.	B
620.	C
621.	B
622.	B
623.	C
624.	B
625.	C

Set 26

626.	B
627.	B
628.	A
629.	C
630.	C
631.	B
632.	A
633.	B
634.	B
635.	B
636.	A
637.	B
638.	C
639.	D
640.	B
641.	A
642.	A
643.	B
644.	C
645.	C
646.	A
647.	C
648.	B
649.	C
650.	A

Set 27	
651.	C
652.	C
653.	A
654.	B
655.	A
656.	Mr. Willoughby
657.	B
658.	A
659.	B
660.	C
661.	C
662.	A
663.	B
664.	C
665.	C
666.	B
667.	B
668.	A
669.	A
670.	B
671.	B
672.	B
673.	C
674.	B
675.	B

Set 28	
676.	C
677.	C
678.	A
679.	C
680.	A
681.	B
682.	B
683.	B
684.	C
685.	A
686.	A
687.	B
688.	C
689.	B
690.	C
691.	A
692.	C
693.	C
694.	3 (Elinor & Edward, Marianne & Willoughby, Elinor & Col. Brandon)
695.	A
696.	C
697.	A
698.	A
699.	B
700.	A

Set 29	
701.	B
702.	A
703.	A
704.	A
705.	B
706.	A
707.	B
708.	C
709.	B
710.	Isabella Thorpe
711.	B
712.	C
713.	A
714.	A
715.	A
716.	C
717.	A
718.	A
719.	B
720.	A
721.	C
722.	A
723.	A
724.	B
725.	A

Set 30	
726.	C
727.	A
728.	C
729.	A
730.	B
731.	B
732.	B
733.	C
734.	A
735.	C
736.	B
737.	C
738.	A
739.	C
740.	C
741.	B
742.	C
743.	C
744.	A
745.	A
746.	B
747.	A
748.	B
749.	A
750.	C

About the authors

Tiffany Bascom is a counselor and devoted Janeite.

Trudy Wallis is an ESL teacher and author of the novel *Longbourn Library* as well as the forthcoming *Norland Castle*.

www.ingramcontent.com/pod-product-compliance
Lightning Source LLC
Chambersburg PA
CBHW051503170626
46811CB00002B/619